BEFORE THE *lie*

CONFESSION DUET

KD Robichaux

Before the Lie Production Crew

Editing by Hot Tree Editing
www.hottreeediting.com

Cover Design and
Formatting by Pink Ink Designs
www.pinkinkdesigns.com

Cover Photography by FuriousFotog
www.onefuriousfotog.com

Cover Model: Matthew Hosea

Note:
This story is not suitable for persons under the age of 18.

*Potential triggers lie within this book

Also by KD Robichaux

The Blogger Diaries Trilogy:
Wished for You
Wish He was You
Wish Come True
The Blogger Diaries Trilogy Boxed Set

Standalones:
No Trespassing

Anthologies:
Tempting Scrooge

The Confession Duet:
Before the Lie
Truth Revealed (Coming Soon)

BEFORE THE *lie*

EFORE THE *lie*

BEFORE THE *lie*

RE THE *lie*

lie

BEFORE THE LIE

Rosa,
Confession time?

♥♥ Robideaux

BEFORE THE *lie*

EFORE THE *lie*

BEFORE THE *lie*

RE THE *lie*

lie

Prologue

A HAND CLAMPS OVER MY mouth, and his full weight presses against my face, shoving my head into the pillow.

I had been dead asleep, but I'm fully awake now, panic rising within me like lava to the surface, wanting to burst forth through a scream that has no way out.

I claw at his arm, twisting my hips beneath him, but it only seems to help him remove my leggings and underwear, as he yanks at them with his free hand.

So fucking strong. I can't push him off.

My legs. My legs are my biggest source of strength. If I can just....

Naked from the waist down, still pinned in place by the hand over my mouth, I bring my feet up and push my heels against his bare hips, kicking with all my might.

It does nothing.

He rotates his pelvis enough to dislodge my feet and works his body between my thighs. No matter how hard I try to keep them clamped together, I'm no match for the man on top of me.

I begin to cry, realizing this is going to happen. No matter how hard I fight, I will not be able to stop him.

I shouldn't be here.

I only stayed because of the story my husband told me, about his girlfriend in high school who died when she vomited in her sleep. I grew up sheltered, without any alcohol in the house. I drank nothing my whole life except for a sip of wine every Sunday at church during communion. So in my head, liquor was bad. It brought nothing but bad.

My friend had been drinking, and with that damn story in my head, I couldn't very well leave my friend alone. What if it happened to him?

So I stayed. So I could be there to wake him up if he got sick in his sleep.

And now, as he shoves himself inside me, ripping me open as I wail behind his hand...

I wish I'd just left him to die.

One

Vi

Three years earlier...

I'M HANGING ON BY THE TIPS of my fingers and my big toes, clinging with a strength no one really thinks I have until they see it with their own two eyes. I feel a single drop of sweat trickle its way from my hairline, down my temple and cheek, until it finally drops off my jaw. Breathing in deep through my nose, the familiar and comforting scent of rubber I've grown to love fills my lungs. I breathe it out through my mouth before sucking it in once more as I make my move. With a burst of energy shooting me skyward, I leap from my perch on the crimper rocks screwed to the 90-degree wall and dyno to the much larger handgrip three feet above my head, grabbing onto it with perfect timing before finding two more to rest my toes on once again.

The dyno. A move in rock climbing that takes an obscene

amount of practice. It's a leap of faith, basically. You jump, hoping your grip lands on its targeted rock with enough strength to catch yourself with one hand before you fall to your death, or in this case, to the regrind—ground up recycled tires—that cushion your landing.

The smell of rubber, sweat, and hand chalk permeates the rock gym I call my home away from home. I wake up early every morning to shower it out of my hair, where it's clung to me and followed me home, only for it to reattach itself that same afternoon. The eight hours of sleep I get each night, solid and restful from the physical exhaustion I earn every evening, followed by the seven hours I spend at my high school finishing up my senior year, are the only hours during the course of a day that I don't spend here, at Rock On rock gym. It's only six minutes away from school, and fifteen from home, and the only reason I leave at night is because they close and lock down the place at 9:00 p.m. So for six blissful hours each day—from the moment the last bell rings, until the owners of the gym, Mr. and Mrs. Burrell, flash the overhead fluorescent lights to signal closing time—I get to spend it in my happy place, the only place in the world where I actually feel accomplished, good at something. No... amazing, truly talented at something.

It was by pure coincidence we discovered my hidden talent. My first boyfriend, Jax, invited me to go rock climbing with him here for one of our first dates when we were freshmen. At first, I didn't want to go. I'm the least athletic person on the face of the planet. At that point in time, I couldn't touch my toes. PE was a joke. I purposely forgot my gym clothes most of the time so I could just do health assignments instead of participating in class, and when it was time for testing, I would walk the mile run.

I always felt awkward and gangly, with my long, skinny arms and legs, and I was embarrassed to do anything physical in front of my classmates.

So no, I didn't want to go with my super cute blond-haired, blue-eyed boyfriend to the place he spent so many hours at after school. I couldn't understand why he liked it either. He was kinda nerdy like me. But rather than loving books and English class like I did, he preferred computers, and his giant bass in band. After his mother called mine to confirm mutual permission for this date, even my mom tried to reason with me.

"Vi, baby, you might like it. You should try everything once. You never know. You gave up on piano lessons and ballet class, and you haven't signed up to do any more plays after the one you did in eighth grade. So at least go see what this rock climbing stuff is all about," she persisted.

In the end, it was Jax's sister, Maddy, who talked me into going. She loved it as much as he did, and she was my body type, long-limbed and bony, not an ounce of muscle on her scrawny yet tall frame. "I don't like sports," she confessed, "but I love climbing. No balls flying at your face. No running. Just you and the rocks, at your own pace and skill level."

So I gave in. There were no buses at our private school, so when my mom picked me up from school on that crisp winter day, we followed Jax's mom's car until we arrived at the brick building just a few minutes away. The sign at the top looked like a man hanging from the roof by his hand and a harness, the bold letters next to him spelling out *Rock On* with a picture of the well-known hand signal of a pinky and forefinger pointing upward. I grabbed my bag containing the stretch pants and T-shirt Maddy told me to bring to change into out of our school uniform of white polo shirt and khaki dress pants. The four of us—my mom, Jax, Maddy, and me—made our way in through the glass door, the bell attached to the top jamb ringing loudly to announce our presence. Jax waved at his mom as she drove out of the lot. Apparently, she just dropped them off every day, and picked them up at whatever time they set.

It was the smell that hit me first. It was overwhelming. It smelled like the place my parents always went when they had to get new tires, but it was mixed with body odor and something else I couldn't put my finger on. I could feel it in the air though, like the oxygen itself was coating my skin.

Then I took in the interior of the massive structure. It was like they had taken a gutted warehouse and then built random giant foot-thick, ceiling-high walls throughout the space, and then poked holes all over them. Half the holes I saw were covered with multi-colored handholds. Most of the walls stood straight up, but others were angled, and as I peeked around one of the huge straight ones, I saw that the outer edge of the building was lined with one continuous wall of various angles and depths, and it led to a cave, an *actual* cave. Even its ceiling was covered in colorful rocks.

We walked up to the front desk, which was really a long glass display case that showcased all sorts of equipment. I had no idea what any of it was used for. Behind the middle-aged woman greeting us with a friendly smile, there was a wall of shoeboxes, racks of T-shirts, harnesses, cute little colorful bags, and rope.

"Hey, kiddos. Y'all brought a new friend today, I see. How are you, sweetheart?" she asked, turning to me, and I gave her a nervous smile.

"I'm pretty good. Just a little scared," I admitted, and she waved one hand, pushing a clipboard toward my mom, while Jax and Maddy signed their names on another.

"Oh, there's nothing to be scared of. This is meant to be fun. And if you listen to your friends and follow their instructions, they'll teach you how to not hurt yourself," she told me, pointing a pen at my boyfriend and his sister. "Now, if you want to learn to belay, just come and let me know. It's ten dollars for the twenty-minute class and includes rental of one harness for the student." When I looked at her confused, she chuckled. "Getting ahead of myself, hun. That's only if you want to get on the ropes and climb up, not over."

"Think we're just going to boulder today, Mrs. Burrell," Jaxon told her, and to me, he clarified, "That's when you climb sideways, just a little bit up the wall. No ropes or anything. There's a line marking all the walls at eight feet. Not allowed to go up past that without being in a harness."

I nodded then watched my mom sign her name at the bottom of the waiver after filling out all our information. She handed the clipboard back to Mrs. Burrell then smiled at me, rubbing my back briefly when she saw the nerves clearly written all over my face. *Fun*, she mouthed, and I rolled my eyes before shaking my head.

"Come on, Vi! Let's go get changed," Maddy called, skipping toward a set of bathrooms in the corner, so I took hold of my bag and followed after her.

An hour later, with my rented climbing shoes on my feet and chalk bag tied around my waist, dangling over my butt like a tail, and after some simple instructions, like correct foot position—always with the inside of your foot facing the wall—all my nervousness had disappeared and was replaced by a sense of assuredness. Mrs. Burrell even came over to where my mom was sitting on the worn-out, chalk-covered couch in the center of the gym, and I overheard her say that I was a natural. I was damn near keeping up with Jax and Maddy, although they stopped frequently to teach me better techniques to make getting across the wall even simpler for me.

That was the whole thing. I discovered rock climbing didn't require that much strength if you had technique. And with my long reach and small body weight, bouldering was easy enough not to be discouraging, but challenging enough that I wanted to conquer it. Jax told me that climbing upward would be a different story. Technique would still be a big part of it, but I'd need to work on my strength just to be able to pull my body weight up to the next rock. Luckily, I had pretty strong legs from the years of ballet I had taken, but gave up on when I got too self-conscious to wear a leotard in front of people. So until I had more power in my upper body, I could use my legs to push myself up when I needed to.

By the end of the night, I was hooked, and seeing how much fun I had, my mom went ahead and paid for a monthlong membership after I promised I would make use of it. That monthly membership eventually turned into a yearly one, and here it was four years later.

Jaxon and I had broken up just a few months after I started climbing. We realized we were great friends, but there wasn't anything there as far as chemistry. Whatever chemistry could be had by fourteen-year-olds. We continued to climb together often, but where he was ambitious about climbing outdoors, I really had no desire to leave the gym. The rocks changed positions every couple of months, so the routes were always different. And

I still preferred bouldering to climbing, no hindrances of ropes and harnesses, just me, the walls, and my Prana chalk bag—a Christmas gift from my big brother. I loved it as much as if he handed me a Louis Vuitton.

The bells over the door jingle on the other side of the gym, pulling me out of my memories. I don't look over to see who it is, figuring it's just another one of the regulars who will come say hi to me after they sign in. Instead, I walk to the wall directly in front of that same old worn-out, chalk-covered couch my mom is sunk into, where she's reading the latest Nora Roberts book. Even after all this time, she refuses to just drop me off. She stays the whole time, six hours a day, my biggest fan and greatest cheerleader. She even learned to belay soon after I made climbing a hobby I was going to stick with. So whenever I'm going up on the ropes, she puts on her own harness, hooks herself to the line and carabiner attached to the floor. One end of the rope loops through an anchor in the top of the rock wall that threads through her belay device, and she'll wait for me to tie my own harness to the other end of the same rope. We've done it so many times now that we do it more through mindless muscle memory than anything else. I can't even count how many 8-knots I've tied in the last four years.

"Momma, mark me," I call over to her, and hand her a piece of sidewalk chalk when she walks over to where I stand in front of the wall.

"Any requests?" she asks, making her way to the far left end of the blue-painted wall, which already has tons of markings all over it from people making their own routes.

"Hmmm... I need to practice squatted positions, so make it a low route," I tell her, and she begins circling hand and foot holds until she's all the way to the right end of the wall.

"There you go, doll." She hands me back the chalk stick, and I put it in my chalk bag dangling over my butt, reaching in farther to coat one hand and then the other in the sweat-absorbing powder.

"Thanks, Mom. That middle part is going to be a bitch," I point out, biting the inside of my cheek and trying to figure out how I'm going to make it from one set of crimpers (tiny rocks you can only grasp with your fingertips) to another without any jugs or mini-jugs (larger rocks that are easy to grab with your whole hand) in between.

"You got it. Take your time," she encourages, and I blow out a breath, taking up my start position at the beginning of the route.

I've fallen six times trying to make it from the first set of crimpers to the next, and I'm about to make my seventh attempt, when I hear, "Spidergirl!" yelled from the front of the gym, breaking my concentration, and my left foot slips off its precarious perch on a chip the size of a quarter. I get my legs under me just in time to land in a squat rather than on my ass.

"Dammit," I hiss, but then out loud, I reply, "Yeah, Sierra?"

"We have two newbs. Will you give them their belay lessons, please? I'd do it, but I'm in the middle of feeding little man his dinner." Sierra is the owners' daughter-in-law. She runs the office in the evenings now, and instead of putting her new baby in day care, she just brings him along with her to work. I spend lots of my breaks holding the adorable little guy. I don't work here, but I'm a part of the climbing team, so we often give the belay lessons to people who sign up for them. An actual employee just has to give them a final test before the climber earns their certification.

"Coming!" I call, and start making my way to the front, clapping and rubbing my hands together to shake off the remaining chalk. I'm almost near the entrance, when the tingling in my nose starts, and as it creeps up the back of my eyes, I know it's going to be a doozy. I stop where I am, look up into the fluorescent lights, and let it rip. *"Achoo!"* I sneeze, my feet coming off the ground with its force as I cover my face with my hands.

"I'd give that one an eight out of ten," Sierra scores, a long-standing tradition the regulars have when we sneeze from all the chalk in the air.

But then I hear the sexiest deep voice add, "Bless you," and that's when I finally look up at the newbs.

With my hands still covering my face, I peek over my fingers and take in the two men standing at the glass display case that Sierra is currently behind, baby Alaric hidden beneath a nursing blanket with just his tiny feet poking out. One of the men is super tall, probably 6'5", with a military haircut and kind eyes. But my eyes only land on him briefly before they lock on the ones belonging to his friend.

My heart pounds in my chest and I can't seem to take in enough oxygen as I watch his dark brown eyes trail down my body. His gaze travels from the top of my high ponytail to the black toes of my climbing shoes then back up to meet my green eyes, still the only thing visible of my face behind my palms. He's not tall, especially compared to his friend, maybe just a couple inches taller than me, but his body, dressed in a black wife beater, basketball shorts, and tennis shoes, looks like it was chiseled by Michelangelo himself.

Tattoos cover his arms and the upper part of his chest I can see above the neck of his shirt, and his head is shaved. But with as much as there is to take in, it's those gorgeous chocolate eyes that hold my attention. They're sucking me in, and I can't for the life of me look away or even move.

It's not until Sierra chuckles "She says thank you" that I finally snap out of it.

"Umm... hold that thought," I say, and jog to the bathroom in the corner. I get some tissue and blow my nose, and then wash my hands at the sink, glancing at myself in the mirror.

Jesus, I look horrendous. I have white streaks of chalk from my scalp down to my knees, and the mascara I put on this morning before school seems to be everywhere but on my eyelashes from sweating. I wet a paper towel and clean up the black smudges, but as I take in my red tank top and black spandex shorts, I know there's really nothing else I can do for my appearance.

I have no idea what I'm so worried about. I've never cared before what other people thought of my looks while I'm here in my happy place. It's the one place I'm never self-conscious. In my head, it doesn't matter what I look like, because my confidence in my talent radiates outward and disguises the fact I look like I crawled out of a swamp.

But that guy out there... I have never before experienced what I felt under his gaze. What the hell was that? Part of me wants to hide in the bathroom until I can sneak out and escape past them, but another part wants to hurry up and dry my hands so I can get back out there to *him*. Knowing there would be no way to signal my mom sitting on the other side of the gym if I tried to make a run for it, I go with the second option, using a couple paper towels before tossing them in the trashcan and yanking open the bathroom door.

When I get back to everyone, the guys are sitting on a bench in the shop area, lacing up their rental shoes. I walk behind the counter and grab my harness from where I keep it in one of ten cubbies reserved for the competition climbing team, carrying it over to the shop.

The tall one finishes first and looks up at me where I stand a few feet away. "Damn, that thing is way cooler than the one I've got," he jokes, holding up the plain black rental harness.

I smile, and look down at my personal harness in my hand. Another gift from my older brother, Henry. He was so excited when he learned that his baby sister was really getting into a sport that he went all out and got me a chalk bag, harness, and top of the line climbing shoes so I could stop renting the ones here at Rock On. He told me, "Now that you have all your own gear, you're a *real* climber, and you can't just give up on it like you did everything else." I had rolled my eyes but attacked his cheek with a hundred kisses, thanking him profusely.

The gear didn't come cheap. The harness is thickly padded around the waist and legs, and is obscenely comfortable, even while hanging for long periods of time. It's black on the outside and neon purple on the inside, with the same purple color thread stitched throughout the black. My climbing shoes are pure black brushed leather, streamline and sleek, fitting my feet like a glove. They feel almost like a soft-sole moccasin, but they lace up the top like a tennis shoe and have thick and hard places along the toes and outside edges. The shoes bend with your feet, but also protect them when pressed into a rock. You don't wear socks with your climbing shoes, which equals the stench of "sweaty pedis" as Sierra calls them, hence the never-ending supply of Lysol on the counter near the shoe drop-off table.

"Don't worry. Yours will still keep you up on the rope. Your junk just won't be as comfortable," I reply to Tall Guy, and he laughs, holding out his hand.

"Glover. Nice to meet you...." he prompts.

"Glover? Oh, you're military, huh? That's your last name?" I ask, placing my hand in his. We get quite a few Army guys in here for PT, since our small town is right next to Ft. Vanter, but I've never really hung out with anyone in the military except for Henry, who is in the Navy, stationed in Charleston.

"Oh, yeah. Sorry. Haven't been out in the civilian world that much in the past year. I was just stationed here right out of boot camp. Haven't used my first name in a while. I'm Brian," he tells me, and I smile.

"Nice to meet you, Brian. I'm Vivian, but most people call me Vi." As I pull my hand from his, his friend comes to stand next to him, and I feel his presence like I've stuck my hand on a doorknob after skidding my socked feet over a carpeted floor. I look down, and sure enough, the blonde hairs on my arms are standing up.

"I'm Corbin," he says, and he holds out his hand.

I hesitate for a moment, scared of what my body's reaction might be if I touch him; it's already acting strange just being near him. But I don't want to seem rude, so I timidly rest my fingers against his palm, and then feel his close around them. My breath catches as my heart stops for a moment, then restarts as if I've been shocked back to life. I feel his warmth blanket every cell of my body, along with a sense of excitement coated in complete calm. "H... hi."

All I can do is stand there, my hand in his, and I stare into those intense, mesmerizing dark eyes, entranced by the feelings roiling through me. He seems to be just as hypnotized, his breath coming and going deeply through his flared nostrils.

"Sir," I hear Brian say, seemingly from far away. "Um, Specialist Lowe?"

"Just Corbin," he says, his lips barely moving, his eyes never wavering from mine.

"Okay then. Corbin, you um... Sorry, sir. But uh, you ready to climb?" Brian asks, and a spark of confusion pulls me out of my trance.

My brows lower and I glance up at Brian, who towers over us, then focus back on Corbin. "Sir?" I prompt, and his eyes flare and his hand tightens around mine briefly before letting go.

"Yeah, he's basically my boss. I'm a Private, or a 'cherry' as they keep calling me, and he's a Specialist, three ranks higher than me," Brian explains.

"Oh. Cool. So um, are y'all ready to learn how to belay?" I ask, taking a step back, trying to get a little farther away from the intensity of the man in front of me. This pulls a chuckle from Brian, and my face heats.

"Yeah, little lady. Teach us how to belay," he says, not bothering to hide the sarcasm in his voice.

It strikes a match inside me, slightly offending me, but instead of responding, I decide to save it for the rocks. They may see me as a 'little lady' now, but I'll show them.

BEFORE THE *lie*
BEFORE THE *lie*
BEFORE THE *lie*
RE THE *lie*
lie

Two

Vi

STANDING AT THE BEGINNERS' wall, which is covered in nothing but jug grips, I step into my harness and pull the waist-strap tight, waiting for them to put on their own. I can't help but let my eyes wander over Corbin as he adjusts his thigh straps, pulling at his shorts where they rode up his legs when he pulled his harness up. I assume Brian gets his on fine, but I wouldn't be able to swear on it, because my gaze is like metal, attaching itself to Corbin as if he were a magnet.

"Okay, so who wants to be the belayer, and who wants to be the climber first?" I ask, and Corbin answers, "I'll belay first," coming to stand close to me where I'm holding onto the anchor attached to the floor.

"All right, so this attaches to your harness... um... there," I begin, pointing at the belayer's loop at the front of his harness, feeling my cheeks heat once again. I don't understand what is with me around this guy. Usually, I just snap the carabiner onto the loop, without even thinking about how close it is to someone's... private area. But with him, instead, I hand over the metal shackle with its spring-loaded gate and allow him to hook it on himself. "And it anchors you to the floor. That way if someone much larger than you is climbing, you won't end up trading places in the air."

I move over to Brian, taking hold of one end of the doubled-over rope hanging from its anchor at the top of the rock wall. "Okay, climber." I glance up at Corbin to make sure he's watching, so he'll know what to do when it's his turn, finding his eyes burning into me before lowering them to the rope in my hands. I clear my throat, trying to free my airway, because suddenly it's hard to breathe. "Um... so the climber will take one end of the rope, and measure out enough length that it goes from your fist to your opposite shoulder. So do that," I instruct, and Brian's long wingspan measures out his rope. "Now you tie an 8-knot at that length."

"Oh, I got this," Brian says excitedly, and I watch closely as he ties the rope into a perfect 8-knot.

"Good, now, you thread it through the two horizontal loops that sandwich the vertical belayer's loop. Yep, just like that, and you're going to make your knot into a double by lacing the end of the rope through and following the line of your eight. Perfect. Wow, this is so much easier than teaching a civilian." I laugh, and then add, "Now just finish it off with a safety knot at the top, and you're done." He quickly ties the simple knot above the more intricate one, and his part is complete.

I take the two steps back over to Corbin, dragging the second half of the rope with me. "You have your belay device?" I ask, looking down at his hands.

"No," he replies, and the one word reverberates through me. As little as he's spoken, when he actually does, it's like it sends a shockwave through the air.

"Oh, sorry. Let me go grab one real quick." I jog away, feeling my high ponytail swish across the back of my shoulders. Sensing eyes on me, I glance over my shoulder, and sure enough, Corbin's are once again boring into me. But this time, they're on my ass. The realization makes my step falter, and I nearly trip, but luckily I'm close enough to the glass case that I catch myself with my palms to the edge.

He's checking me out? The thought makes me both giddy and nervous. I haven't had a boyfriend since Jax and I broke up our freshman year, and with graduation just a few months away, the comments of the assholes at school who have picked on me mercilessly for never dating come to the surface of my brain.

She's such a snob. She doesn't think anyone is good enough for her.

What a dork. She'd rather go to that stupid gym than come to the Fall Dance.

What guy would want a girl who spends all her time climbing on walls?

All she does is talk about that rock climbing crap.

My mom comforts me when their words finally penetrate the armor I've been able to build around myself with the confidence I've gained since finding my niche. She calls them jealous and immature. In reality, I know she's happy I've spent the last four years of my life in love with a sport instead of chasing after boys.

But the fact is, it's left me completely inexperienced with the opposite sex. Jax and I had kissed a few times, but never with tongue. So here I am, eighteen years old and soon to graduate high school, and I have never even French kissed before.

So catching Corbin looking at my butt in my spandex climbing shorts is brand new territory for me. Territory I don't even know how to explore, so I decide to tuck it into a hidden nook in my brain so I can try to forget about it until absolutely necessary.

Reaching into the display case, I grab a belay device and hurry back over to Corbin, finding it impossible to look him in the eyes. "Y'all probably already know this, but I have to do my spiel. This is a tubular belay device. It attaches to the belayer's harness in the front by a locking carabiner."

My hands tremble, but I'm determined to act like I normally would with any other person taking the belay lesson, so I rotate the metal lock on the clip, and hook it onto the loop at the front of his hips. Being this close, his soft shorts tucked close against his body because of the harness, it is impossible to miss the movement of his penis behind the black fabric. I jerk my hands away, my entire body growing flushed and my skin suddenly feeling too tight around my bones. Even my scalp feels hot and prickly.

I've read romance novels before. I'm actually a pretty big fan of paranormal love stories. I don't have much time for reading nowadays, but I've read enough that I get the gist of sex, as much as you can get without actually experiencing it yourself. I've read all about 'twitching members' and 'tight channels', so I know exactly what just happened in Corbin's shorts.

He's affected by me as well.

With wide eyes, I look up into Corbin's. His expression is

unreadable. No cocky smirk, no blush of embarrassment from his body's reaction to me. Whatever emotion he is feeling is completely concealed behind the wall of his heart-stopping, perfect face. So, I clear my throat again and stutter through the next part of their lesson.

"Um... o-okay. S-so next, you grab your rope and pinch it in half, then stick the pinched part through one side of the belay device, so when it comes through the metal, it makes a loop that you will hook onto the locking carabiner too." I watch as Corbin does as I instructed, and when he spins the lock back into place, he looks up at me, waiting for my next step.

"I'm going to hook into the rope next to you so you can watch how I do it," I tell them, making quick work of unhooking my personal belay device from the loop I keep it on at my hip, and then strapping into the rope next to them so I can demonstrate the proper movements. Normally, I would just stand behind the student, wrap my arms around theirs, and teach them that way. But the thought of doing that sends me into near panic.

"Before you can climb, the climber and the belayer must let each other know they're ready. The climber will ask, 'On belay?' and the belayer will answer with, 'Belay is on,' if they're all set up. The belayer will then ask the climber if they're ready to start climbing by asking, 'On rock?' and when the climber approaches the wall and is ready to begin, they will respond with, 'Rock on.'" Without thinking, I say the last part while giving the rock-n-roll hand signal, a little growl to my voice out of habit. This makes Brian laugh. When I realize what I did, my eyes lift to Corbin, and I see one side of his lips is lifted, his dark eyes twinkling. I've given these instructions so many times, usually to kids and their parents, and I'm so used to trying to make it fun and calm their nerves that I always say the last reply to the belayer that way. Seeing the guys' reaction to my dramatics, my embarrassment doesn't have a chance to form, so I chuckle along with Brian. "Okay, y'all's turn."

Brian clears his throat animatedly, and then holds his hand palm up in Corbin's direction, asking, "On belay, sir?"

Corbin shakes his shaved head and runs a palm down his face. "You're such an idiot. Belay is on, cherry." Brian laughs and moves up to the wall. "On rock?" Corbin asks him.

Brian places one hand on a grip, and then looks over at me, his other hand copying my rock-n-roll gesture, as he growls loudly, "Rock on!" making me laugh at his antics.

"Very good," I tell them. "And now you can climb. As he moves up the wall, the rope is going to get slacker. With your right hand, you are going to pull the slack out of the line through the belay device. Between his moves, you lock off the rope by just pulling it in your right hand down by your hip. If he warns you he is about to fall, or if he falls without warning, he's not going anywhere if you already have him locked off. The only time you are not in the locked off position is if you are pulling out his slack."

"Got it," Corbin replies, watching me demonstrate pulling my empty rope through the device and locking it off as I instructed.

"Did you get all that, Brian?" I ask, and he nods from his perch on the first set of beginner rocks.

"Awesome," Sierra says, coming up behind me, and I smile over at her. She stays with our little group while Brian goes up the wall then lets go, letting Corbin practice catching him a couple times before lowering him to the ground one final time. They switch places, Corbin becoming the climber and Brian the belayer, and ten minutes later, they receive their certification.

"I'm going to get back to my route. Nice meeting you guys. Have fun," I tell them, and with an awkward little wave, I go back to the wall in front of my mom who's sitting on the couch. She's still reading her book, completely unaware of the emotional rollercoaster I was just on.

I reach into my chalk bag and coat my hands, then take up my starting position at the left end of the route once again, completely aware of Brian and Corbin choosing the wall across from me. They must not notice, or maybe they don't care, that the wall they picked is marked Expert, as they begin strapping themselves into the ropes. I don't say anything though. They're grown men and will figure it out on their own. Even if it's the hard way.

Corbin

WHAT. THE. FUCK?

Her presence caught my attention before the loud sneeze lifted her small frame off the floor. I had felt the approach of something... someone... as if it were a physical thing. Like the scene in *Jurassic Park*, the water rippling in the glasses as the giant T-Rex grew closer and closer, shaking the ground with its advance. So when I looked over my shoulder where I was standing at the front counter, and my eyes landed on the girl making her way from the back of the gym, clapping her hands together and forming a small dust cloud as she walked, I was struck stupid. Her? She was the one causing this strange feeling inside me?

She didn't look a day over fifteen. Her long, dark ponytail swished behind her as she hurried toward us. When she circled around one of the walls, I took in her thin arms and legs, exposed thanks to the bright red tank top and skin-tight black spandex shorts she was wearing. Her black sports bra peeked out from beneath her shirt, but it didn't seem like she needed it. Her chest was small, in proportion with the rest of her. But God, she was stunningly beautiful, her face clear of makeup except for the smudge of black around her eyes, and the chalk smeared on her cheeks, forehead, and the tip of her nose.

And then she had sneezed, and my automatic reaction to say, "Bless you," brought her eyes to mine, and it felt like I was being electrocuted. I vaguely heard the lady behind the desk say something about her being an eight out of ten, but to me, she far surpassed a dime. She was utterly perfect.

I watched her jog away, the toned muscles of her ass working behind those tiny black shorts, before she disappeared through the door marked Women. I shook myself. I shouldn't be checking out a little teenager. I'm a damn twenty-year-old Specialist in the US Army, soon to be up for my next promotion. That's the last thing I should be doing.

With that thought in mind, I tried to hold myself in check while Glover joked around with her. Glover, the nineteen-year-old Private from Kentucky, was my new cherry. He arrived to my unit a little over two weeks ago, and the poor kid hadn't done anything off base or fun since he'd made it to Ft. Vanter. Part of the job, aside from making sure the people beneath my rank do the right shit and follow orders, is making sure they keep their head straight. Nothing could be more disastrous than a depressed soldier. So when I noticed Glover looking a little down in the chow hall this afternoon, I asked him if he wanted to check out this climbing place I'd seen an ad for in the paper. His eyes had lit up like a Christmas tree, and we made plans to come right after we got off work for the day.

I'd kept myself under control as she gave us the first of the required instruction before we could be tested and certified for belaying. But when her hands came so fucking near my cock to hook the locking carabiner onto my harness, I couldn't control its natural reaction as it swelled and practically reached for her. All I could do was keep my face stoic, as if nothing had happened, even as she looked up at me, her breathtaking green eyes startled, confirming she hadn't missed my dick twitch.

Then, I couldn't help but smile when her tiny fist had lifted, and her pointer and pinky fingers shot up, her sweet, feminine voice deepening to a far from intimidating growl as she taught us the verbal cues to start climbing, ending with, "Rock on." A tiny bit of her true personality had shone through her nervousness around me. And I could tell it was just around me. She didn't seem affected by Glover—yet I hadn't missed the flare of her nostrils and the brief narrowing of her eyes when he laughed after she asked if we were ready to learn how to belay.

That had pissed her off. Most people probably wouldn't have picked up on that, but it's my job to read people, notice the tiniest of changes in their demeanor. And if his condescending tone had pissed her off, then that meant she was probably pretty good at what she did, and knew it. That, and the fact the lady at the front desk called her Spidergirl.

Now, as I belay Glover—trying his best to make it up a wall

that looks nearly impossible, since it has so few rocks on it, and the rocks that *are* screwed in don't look big enough to hold up a toddler, much less a fucking 6'5" man like him—I watch her in action. I see exactly why Vi would have been offended by him laughing in her face. I can also see the reason she would own the nickname Spidergirl.

Staying down low on the wall, never standing up straight to reach a rock above her head, I see she's only using rocks that have been circled in chalk, so she must be practicing a certain route. She starts at the far left side of the wall and places the outside of her left foot onto the first bottom rock, puts all of her weight on it, and she squats to place both hands on a larger grip, her arms outstretched. Her right leg comes up straight in front of her, running parallel with the wall. She doesn't place her right foot on a rock; she just seems to press it against the textured wall itself.

Taking a deep breath, when she lets it out, she pulls herself forward, her left foot somehow spinning on its tiny rock so that it's now her big toe pressed into it. Now, with the front of her body flush with the wall, her right leg stretches far enough to reach the next circled rock and her right hand grasps another. Observing her from this distance, right now, she looks as if she's in a deep side-lunge, yet I know she's somehow balanced on just a sliver of a foothold, making it look effortless.

Bringing her left hand to grip onto the same rock as her right, her tight ass juts out for a moment as she switches which leg her weight is on, now in a lunge to the right. Slowly, she outstretches her arms again, leaning away from the wall instead of holding herself tightly to it. It's fascinating to watch. So slight, so frail, as if there is no strength in her lithe limbs, yet she moves across the wall so gracefully, almost like she's floating.

A couple moves later, she reaches the spot where she's fallen several times since she finished with our belay lesson. It had been her hissed, "Shit!" that brought my eyes to her after I'd hooked myself into the floor anchor ten minutes ago.

Until now, I had been unconsciously belaying Brian as I watched her, my eyes never leaving her, but still completely aware of my soldier up on the ropes. We learned and practiced rope work and rappelling until we could do it in complete darkness, using only the tension in the rope as a guide. So yes, although the idea of the young woman *teaching* us to belay was laughable, I hadn't, because I never show my cards in a game of poker. I never know who I'll come across that may be better at something than me, someone I can learn from, even if I have experience in it. Also, I never know when I might win in a fight by tricking the enemy into thinking I'm helpless. Maybe that's a fucked-up way of thinking, not being an open person, but with the life I've led, it's the only way I've survived.

As he calls, "Falling," down to me, I lock him off until he lets go of the wall, then lower him without ever looking away from Vi, silently rooting her on in my head to make it past the part where she keeps slipping off.

She reaches for the miniature grip, thinks better of it, sticking her right hand into her bag for a fresh coat of chalk, and then places her fingertips on the rock once more. I watch, completely entranced, as she gently lays her cheek against the wall and slowly, ever so carefully, lets go with her left hand, bringing it behind her back to cover it in more chalk as well. Focusing in on her legs and ass, I can see the sleek muscles beneath her smooth skin flex and release, minute adjustments she probably doesn't even realize she's making as she keeps her balance in a near split.

This time, I hold my breath, shushing Brian with a raised fist before he even says a word at my side. The tension crackles in the air as we watch her, waiting for her to make her move. And finally, in one fluid transition, her body contorts until her left foot is where her right just was. She's pinching the tiny rock in her left hand now, and without another foothold, she hooks the top of her right foot around the edge of the wall. One last movement of her hands to a much larger rock at the far end, and she's done it.

She leaps off the wall and twirls with a whoop, the woman on the couch I noticed when we first walked over standing to high-five her then rub her back. Vi's face beams, her smile so wide I can see almost every single one of her perfectly white, straight teeth. Gorgeous. Absolutely gorgeous in all her pride at finally beating her self-given challenge.

Suddenly, both women's eyes move in our direction as Brian starts clapping, yelling "Freakin' awesome!" from our position at the wall across from them. Vi laughs and gives him a small wave before her eyes come to me, where I'm still staring in utter fascination.

"You want to climb now, Lowe?" Brian asks, and I pull my gaze away from her to look up at where he towers over me.

"It's Corbin. We're off the clock, bud," I tell him, wanting it to sink in that I've brought him here to have fun. We aren't Specialist and Private right now. We're just two guys hanging out after work. He needs to let loose a little so the stress of our job doesn't get to him, the way it looked like it was beginning to this afternoon at lunch. "Yeah, I'll give it a shot," I add, unhooking the belay device from my harness and trading it for his end of the rope.

Once I'm all tied in, I start my climb. It's slow-going, as I look for rocks big enough to grip onto. When I saw the sign marking this wall Expert, I'd blown it off. How hard could it be? But now that I'm up here, trying to power through this route, I realize I made a big mistake.

My arms are trembling as I hang on to one of the largest rocks on the wall, which is only about the size of a golf ball, when suddenly I hear that sweet voice call up to me, "Lean away from the wall, Corbin," and I glance down to see Vi standing beside Brian. Her hands rest on her hips and she's tilting her head up to look at me.

"What?" Does she want me to come down?

"Lean away from the wall," she repeats. "You're trying to muscle your way up the wall, and you can't do that on this route. Grip that rock with one hand instead of both, and then slowly lean back, straightening out your arm."

I do what she tells me, gripping the small hold with my right hand before leaning back. I take the opportunity to shake out my left arm, dipping my hand into my chalk bag. "Now what?" I ask her, when my biceps aren't shaking and I have circulation back in both arms.

"Now find some rocks to get your feet up on... no, don't turn your feet in. Always climb with your toes pointing outward. Never use the outside unless you're in starting position or if it's completely necessary. There you go. Bring your feet up as far as you can get them. That way you can just stand up to the next set of rocks above your head. No need to wear those big muscles out if you don't really need to use them," she calls, and I can't help the smile that pulls at my lips.

She's so small, and young, and had been so nervous around me up front. But here, in her element, having just conquered a challenge she had been working on tirelessly, her confidence is shining through, and she's feeling brave enough to try and help me, even though my dumb ass thought I'd be able to simply He Man my way up an Expert-level wall.

I bring my feet up as she instructed, still holding on with just one hand. "Go slow. Don't stand up too—"

But her warning is too late. Standing up on the tiny rocks the toes of my climbing shoes press into, I do it too quickly and my knees hit the wood, causing my feet to slip off the rock chips. I fall only a foot before my harness catches me, the rope yanking the straps tight into the creases between my legs and crotch. Brian lowers me to the ground, and as soon as my feet touch the floor, I jerk on the rope to give me more slack and pull the harness out of my balls.

"Good try. You actually got farther than most newbs would get on an expert-level wall," Vi tells me, and it does a lot to soothe my bruised ego.

"How long have you been doing this?" I ask her, untying my knot.

"Every day for four years. I started when I was a freshman," she replies, taking the rope from me and lacing it through the front of her harness.

Freshman. Four years ago? But she looks so young. It could be because of her fresh face and her petite frame, but I didn't think she could be any more than fifteen. "How old are you?" I question before I can stop myself.

"I'm eighteen."

Fuck.

Three

Vi

IT DIDN'T ESCAPE ME THAT Corbin's quiet and standoffish demeanor changed almost the moment I told him I was eighteen. Or maybe it's because I had just tried to help him with his technique. I'm not sure, but for the last hour, Brian, Corbin, and I have been climbing together, me showing them different fun routes around the gym that were easier than the Expert wall, but still challenging enough for two big, strong soldiers.

It did amazing things for my confidence when I demonstrated a route for them, and they'd clap and whoop for me before trying it themselves. Corbin really listened to everything I tried to teach him, taking it in with a nodding head before putting my instruction into action. Brian was just a big goofball, but he was able to get through most of the routes with his wingspan alone.

The strange feeling I had being near Corbin never went away, but it was easier to ignore when I was joking around with them in between teaching them stuff on the rocks. During Brian's turns, Corbin would stand close to me, his huge tattooed arms crossed over his muscular chest, and every once in a while, his bicep would brush mine, sending tingles throughout my body.

In the middle of explaining something, if I happened to look him in the eyes instead of at the wall we were working on, it would steal my words. I could be in the middle of a sentence and lock gazes with him, and it was like someone pressed pause on my brain. It wasn't until either my mom or Brian snapped us out of it that we continued with the lesson.

By the end of the night, when Sierra flashed the overhead lights, my stomach was hurting from laughing, and I was exhausted from my heart beating like I was running a marathon just being close to Corbin. We all sat on the worn-out couch to take off our shoes, Brian making me laugh once more by taking a whiff of one of his and falling to the floor, pretending he was dead. As funny as he was, and cute in a boy-next-door sort of way, it was Corbin I was unequivocally attracted to. Hell, I had never been more attracted to anyone in my life. And it wasn't just his gorgeous face, chiseled body, or sexy bad-boy tattoos. It was something else altogether. Something I couldn't really name, because it was an emotional connection instead of just a physical attraction.

Whatever it was pulled me to him and made me not want to let go. As tired as I was, I didn't want to leave his presence. I didn't want this night to end. So it was with an internal sigh of relief that I gave Corbin my phone number when he asked me for it, so we could get together again to climb. Out in the parking lot, as I was getting into Mom's car, I heard Brian's, "Bye, Vi! Ha! That rhymes!" before he folded himself into Corbin's dark green Camaro, making me shake my head. Corbin grabbed a black ball cap off his front seat and placed it on his shaved head, squeezing the bill before he waved at me over the roof of his car, and I smiled before closing the door behind me.

Mom and I didn't talk much on the way home. She tried to ask about what I thought of the boys, but I gave her a quick, "They were fun," before going back to replaying the past few hours in my head.

So here I lie, in my lavender-covered, pillow-top twin bed, wide-awake three hours later, still thinking about dark chocolate eyes and tattoos I want to hear the stories behind. I wonder when Corbin will text me, to see when we can climb together again. I really need to go to sleep; I have to be up for school in just six hours. But I just can't shut my brain off.

A half hour of tossing and turning later, my phone chimes, making me jump. When I pick it up off my nightstand, there's a message from a number with a weird area code, and my heart thuds behind my ribs.

I enjoyed meeting and climbing with u. I'll come on Friday if u'll be there. —Corbin

I kick off my covers, reading the message over and over again. *What should I say? Oh God, don't be a dork. Don't sound overly excited that he texted, but don't sound like he's bothering you either.* Jesus, I have no idea what I'm doing.

Me 2. I'll be there!

There. Short and sweet.

A smile tugs at the corners of my lips when my phone chimes

again, and I read his message.

Corbin: Ur still up? I sent u that thinking u'd wake up to it in the morning. Or did I wake u?

Me: Can't sleep. No worries.

Corbin: Me neither... Confession time?

My heart skips. What could he possibly want to confess? How do I even reply to that?

Me: Ok...

A few minutes pass, and I wonder if I said the wrong thing. But then his reply comes through, and I see it just took him a while to type it all out.

Corbin: This evening just keeps playing in my head over and over again. I can't stop thinking about u, and it's kind of freaking me out a little bit. When we first met... nah, never mind. It sounds stupid, and I don't want u to think I'm crazy.

Me: No, tell me! I promise I won't think ur crazy. I can't sleep because I can't get u out of my head either. I mean, the whole night was fun, getting to climb with you guys, but... idk.

Corbin: Well, since u promised. It's like I felt u before I saw u. Something inside me sensed u were there before I laid eyes on u. And I'm not talking about that weird feeling u get like someone is watching u. I mean like, a part of me recognized u before we even met.

Wow. I don't even know how to respond. I know exactly what he's feeling, because I did too. But for him to just come right out and say it? I always thought men played games and pretended like they weren't interested for a while. Maybe that was just all in the movies.

Corbin: U there? I didn't scare u off, did I?

Me: I'm here, just kinda surprised.

Corbin: Surprised about what?

Me: I had the same feeling. I'm just surprised u so readily told me. Aren't guys supposed to play hard to get LOL

Corbin: Can I call u?

A squeak leaves my throat as my eyes widen at my phone. Texting is one thing. I can read what he messages me, and then have time to think about my reply, with the ability to delete it and try again if it doesn't sound right. A phone call though... there is no backspace button.

But that voice. That deep, sexy voice I'd gotten to hear all night, once he finally started speaking. I want to hear it again, so I reply a simple, *Yes*.

My phone rings, and even though I knew he was about to call, it still makes me jump. I press Answer, and hold the cell to my ear. "Hello?"

"Hey, Vi," he says, his voice low, and I hear movement.

"Hey," I reply dumbly, closing my eyes. God, I'm so terrible at this. I hear a door close on his end, and then footsteps echoing. "What are you doing?"

"I'm walking out of the barracks so I don't wake anyone up. I could use some fresh air anyways," he tells me.

"Oh." I pause, and then I have to ask, because I have no idea what he's talking about. "What is a barracks?"

He chuckles. "How long have you lived here? Barracks are like shitty apartments for the military. They're more like dorms, actually. Or what I picture dorms to be like. I wouldn't know, since I didn't go to college."

"Oh, okay. I was born and raised here. But I've never met anyone in the Army before," I explain, listening to another door close and then the sound of him groaning lightly, like he was sitting down.

"Where have you been?" he questions with a light laugh.

"Literally hiding under a rock."

He snorts. "Nice one. But really, you've never met anyone in the Army, even living here your whole life?"

"Nope. I mean… maybe that's the wrong word. I've *met* some at the gym, but never really talked to them aside from giving them their belay lesson. For the past four years, I've gone to school, the gym, home, and repeat," I say quietly, feeling kind of embarrassed at how boring my life is.

"Nothing wrong with dedication, baby girl," he soothes, and his term of endearment makes me smile.

"I guess once I found something I was actually good at, I just stuck with it. I'm loyal like that," I joke.

"Loyalty is good." The tone of his voice makes it seem that simple statement means a lot more to him than he's letting on. "Look, I'm going to cut to the chase, okay?"

I gulp, and then pray he can't hear it through the phone. "O-okay."

"I don't know what this feeling is between us. I've never felt anything like it before. This instant connection before even saying a word to each other. I put it out of my head at first, because I thought you were way too young, but when you told me you're eighteen, I stopped ignoring it, and tonight was one of the best nights I've had in a really long-ass time," he confides, and I realize I'm biting my lip, taking in everything he's saying.

"Me too. And not just a long-ass time. I'm more like… *ever*," I confess, and hear him chuckle.

"If that's been your routine for the past four years, then I believe it. But I'm also jumping the gun here. Do you have a boyfriend, Vi?" he asks, and I barely keep myself from laughing.

"N-no. I don't have a boyfriend," I reply, my voice full of amusement. "If I had a boyfriend, I wouldn't be talking to you at almost one in the morning about the crazy feelings you give me. I haven't had one in four years."

"Crazy feelings?"

"A boyfriend," I clarify.

"Oh." A pause. "And you're eighteen?"

"Yeees..." I drawl.

"So are you... are you a—" He clears his throat, and my face turns hot when I realize what he wanted to ask but stopped himself.

"Yeah," I whisper, and the answer hangs in the air. "So anyways, Friday? I'm there every day. Literally. Sometimes I'll skip Sundays to give my body a rest, but that's rare. I go from 3:00 p.m. when I get out of school until they close at nine." I squeeze my eyes closed at my idiotic rambling.

"Wow, six hours a day. No wonder you're so good. You definitely earned that Spidergirl nickname."

I feel myself glow under his compliment. I roll over on my side, pressing my phone between my ear and pillow. "Thanks. How long have you been in the Army? What do you do?"

"I've been in the Army for almost three years, enlisted when I was seventeen, and left for basic the day I turned eighteen. Got here to Ft. Vander about two years ago. And I'm a sniper," he replies.

"A sniper? Like in the movies?" I ask, intrigued.

"Yep, like in the movies." He chuckles.

"And you've been here for two years?" I breathe, closing my eyes.

"Yeah, right here. In these same barracks."

"All this time, and I didn't even know." My voice holds disappointment. I feel like I've somehow been cheated out of time with him for some reason, which is silly.

"Don't sound so down, baby girl. Everything happens for a reason. We met when we were supposed to. Two years ago, I was still a little shithead, and you were only sixteen," he soothes.

"Still a little shithead?" I prompt, my eyebrows furrowing.

"Yeah. I'm from California. That's where all my family is. In high school, I thought I was a little badass and joined a gang, got in some trouble. Anyways, I got caught, and they gave me the option, either I could go to juvie, and when I turned eighteen I could go straight to jail, *or* I could join the military. I chose the military," he explains, and I suck in a breath.

"What did you do?" I ask, before I can think better of it.

"Ah, that's a story for a different day. I want you to fall for me before I go telling you my deep, dark secrets," he jokes in his deep, sexy voice, and I nearly swoon.

"Fair enough," I breathe.

"Well, I gotta get some sleep. I have to wake up in about three hours for PT, and I know you've got school in the morning. Can I text you tomorrow? Or today, rather. Past midnight, so technically it's Thursday, huh?"

"Of course. If I don't answer right away, I'm in class. It's not so bad having to wait 'til Friday to see you again, when we can technically say it's tomorrow," I say, and I close my eyes and smack my hand over them. Oh, my God, how freaking corny and girly was that?

But his response makes me feel a whole lot less like an idiot. "My thoughts exactly, baby girl. Sleep well."

"Night, Corbin," I whisper, and I hear the phone disconnect.

Corbin

I SIT AT MY DESK like a zombie, hating life and counting down the hours until I can go to sleep, wake up, and it be the day I get to see *her* again. After talking to Vi, I never did fall asleep last night, lying in bed, unable to get her off my mind. Before I could doze off, my alarm went off, at 4:00 a.m. and I had to get up for our daily physical training. Four words kept circling my mind like a mantra I couldn't shut up.

Vivian. Eighteen. Virgin. Mine.

Maybe it was her innocence that made her seem so young when I first met her. I've been with eighteen-year-olds before, both before and after I was that age. Fuck, I lost my own virginity to one when I was fourteen. But they were all already experienced, with an air of maturity surrounding them from the life milestone of sex alone. I wanted her before, but now... now I crave her.

Untouched. Unscarred. No baggage. No one for me to want to kill for having put their hands on what's mine.

And completely moldable.

I scold myself, thinking that way. But really. I could be myself with her, teach her the things I like, no matter how fucked up they are, and she would never know the difference. She wouldn't know that what I wanted... what I *needed*... wasn't the norm.

"For the past four years, I've gone to school, the gym, home, and repeat."

So sheltered. No room for intimate socializing and experimentation with a strict schedule like that. Always under adult supervision, no matter where she went.

"I'm loyal like that."

God, could she be more perfect? Loyalty. The number one thing on my list of requirements.

My deal-breaker. My hard-limit. If you couldn't be fucking loyal to me, then get the fuck away from me. I have zero tolerance for disloyalty. If you're with me, you're with me alone. You could be the most beautiful and most amazing woman on the face of the planet, but the second you break my trust, I don't give a fuck who you are; I'm done with you. I've been burned too many times giving people second chances to ever give another one for the rest of my life. Never again. But for her to use that word, the most important one to me, right there in our very first real conversation? It feels like a higher power is at work.

Combine that with the immediate connection we had before we even spoke, that pull toward each other, that overwhelming sense of needing to be near her, to keep my eyes on her, to touch her, even just by brushing my arm with hers... It felt like fate. I believe in what I told her. Everything happens for a reason.

I've lived here two years. For almost a year of that, I've known about that rock gym she's been going to every single day for almost half a decade, but I never took the time to go check it out. But then yesterday morning, I saw another ad for it in the paper someone had left on the table I sat at for lunch. And with it fresh in my mind, I'd noticed my cherry, Glover, staring into his bowl of canned fruit cocktail, looking like a puppy that had been abandoned. So I invited him to go with me. And there she was.

I can't take it anymore. I've tried to leave her alone, knowing she's at school, but I can't go another minute without texting her. I look out the window behind me to make sure no one is walking up the sidewalk from the parking lot, and seeing the coast is clear, I snatch my phone out of my metal desk drawer and type out a message, pressing send.

Hope u got more sleep than I did. I never fell asleep last night. Awake going on 33 hrs now.

I drop my phone face-up into the drawer in front of me, keeping it cracked open enough so I can look down and see when it lights up, since I have to have it on silent. I'm actually not supposed to have my phone at all while I'm at my desk, but fuck it. There was no way I was going to miss a call or text if Vi decided to send me one. God, so wrapped up in her, and we only met yesterday.

My fingers tap against the top of my desk, and I play a game of solitaire on the ancient computer in front of me. My eyes constantly glance down to see if she responded. I light up my screen a few times to make sure I didn't miss anything while I was looking away, but nothing. When I can feel my sanity starting to slip, my phone finally lights up with Vivian's name.

I feel like a kid on Christmas morning as I open up the message, and I shake my head at myself. The fuck is wrong with me? But I can't help the smile that spreads across my face as I read her text.

I ended up taking a bath to relax, and then finally got about 3 hrs of sleep.

My dick hardens immediately, thinking of her, naked in a bathtub, unable to sleep because she can't stop thinking of me. I reply quickly, hoping she hasn't left her phone yet.

Are u trying to torture me at work?

My smile widens at her response.

Huh? What do u mean? I just got to Chemistry. Cool teacher, so we can text all we want.

God, so innocent. I check the time, seeing that everyone will still be at lunch for another twenty minutes unless they decide to leave early.

Just thinking about u taking a bath, baby girl.

She takes a couple minutes to respond, and when she does, it makes me chuckle.

Oh.

But then I frown when I realize she still doesn't get what I was trying to say, and growl at her follow-up text.

Thinking of me naked is torture? I don't look that bad, do I?

I close my eyes and take a deep breath, letting it out slowly to calm myself before I write her back.

Vivian, I will tell u this 1 time, and 1 time only. Save this message to reread as u see fit if u have to, because this is the only time I will type out these words. U are fucking perfect. There is not a single thing about ur body that I would change. Never doubt I wouldn't kill to see and touch every inch of ur perfection. No, thinking of u naked isn't torture because u look bad. It's torture, because I have the most painful hard-on right now, thinking of u naked, and there's nothing I can do about it.

I try to relax, reminding myself she's inexperienced with the opposite sex, and even less experienced with someone like me. Her short reply comes a few minutes later.

Oh. I'm sorry.

I groan. So. Fucking. Perfect. No excuses. No defensiveness. No arguing. Just an apology. The only thing that could've made it better was if she had said it wouldn't happen again, topped off with a "Sir." God, when she called me that, her tiny hand gripped in mine when we first introduced ourselves, I could barely contain myself. My hand had tightened around hers, ready to yank her to me, so I quickly let go.

I can't wait to see you tomorrow. I'm going to try to get off early so I can get there around the same time you do. Give us more time together.

Her response comes quickly, eager to latch onto my change in subject.

I can't wait either! Will Brian be coming too? We'll have to play takeaway.

The only thing I want to take away is everyone and everything separating us, including her clothes. But not wanting to scare her, my reply is much more G-rated.

Looking forward to u teaching me takeaway. IDK if Glover will come. He told me this morning that he's sore as fuck.

I actually laugh out loud at her incoming text. Knowing she's so tiny makes it even funnier, coming from her.

What a wimp. Tell him to quit being a baby.

My watch beeps, letting me know it's a new hour, which means people will soon be walking in the door.

I'll do that. I gotta get back to work for now, but I'll talk to u later, ok?

I don't get to see if she replies, because the door next to me opens and I swiftly hide my phone in the drawer, shutting it silently.

Three hours later, I'm in my barracks room, lying in my single bed. My roommate was deployed two months ago for an eighteen-month stint in Afghanistan, so I have the place all to myself. As you enter, my bed is in the corner, pushed up against the left wall next to the door. I look around, seeing only the backsides of two floor-to-ceiling wardrobes, one at the foot of my bed, and one to my right, making an opening just big enough to get into the enclosed haven I've created with the furniture, and just wide enough to peek out through to watch the TV sitting on a dresser across the room.

My eyes move to the ceiling, counting the tiny holes in the tiles. As exhausted as I am from not sleeping last night, I still can't shut my brain off, even now, when I can finally pass the fuck out. The image of a small, almost frail girl with long dark hair, green eyes, and a smile that lights up an entire room won't clear itself from the backs of my eyelids.

God, the things I could do to her. The positions I could put her in. It would be effortless. And now, knowing that if I were to take her, I would be her first... it's not even the virgin-aspect that's so fucking hot about it. It's the fact that I would be the one to set the baseline, the standard, for anyone after me. She would always remember me, as her first. She would always compare everyone else to me. The thought makes me both hard and want to punch something, just thinking about anyone else having her. Because another thought hits me.

If I were to have her, and things worked out between us, I would get to live my life knowing I was the only man to ever be inside her.

Before I realize what I'm doing, I take my throbbing cock in my hand, stroking it from tip to root then back up again, already feeling wetness at the head. I didn't allow myself to jack off last night, no matter how badly I'd needed to come. I refused to let myself give in, knowing it was Vi who controlled my thoughts and need, and not me. She'd taken over without my permission, without even trying, just by simply… existing. And to both my relief and distress, I come within seconds.

I clean myself off and lie there for a few minutes, willing myself to go to sleep, but as I realize the sweet bliss of unconsciousness is still not coming, it makes me angry, and my anger brings me to my feet, where I pull on some basketball shorts and a fresh wife beater before lacing up my sneakers.

I grab my keys, glancing at my watch—6:37 p.m. Without thinking, I hop in my Camaro and head off base. Ten minutes later, I pull in and park, slamming the door behind me. I barrel through the glass entrance, making the bells above the door clang violently, and it does wonders to calm the raging bull inside me, the girl currently halfway up the rope two walls over being the red matador's cape.

My loud entrance startles her, and she loses her footing for a moment, but quickly recovers before looking through the space between her lifted right arm and her body to see who had come in, her face annoyed. When she sees it's me, her features soften before breaking out in a wide smile.

And just like that, all frustration leaves me and I'm left with a sense of completeness just being in the same room as her. "Evening, Spidergirl," I call up to her.

"Howdy, soldier," she giggles. "Be right down." Instead of letting go of her grips though, she resumes her focus, and I watch, fascinated, as she finishes her route to the top, making the Expert level wall look effortless in her grace. "Falling," she calls to her mom, who begins letting out slack, allowing her daughter to lower.

On her descent, making my heart stop for a moment, Vi lets go of the rope with her hands and lies back, her body completely horizontal except for her dangling legs as she shakes out her arms. Sensing her nearness to the ground, she grasps the rope in one hand and pulls herself back up just as her feet touch the floor, and then unties her harness before slipping that down her long, bare legs.

She hands it to her mom, kissing her cheek and whispering something I can't hear before finally coming to me. "What are you doing here? It's not Friday yet." She smiles shyly.

"Honestly, I have no idea. I went to bed as soon as I got off work at five, couldn't sleep, and next thing I knew, I was here," I confess, taking hold of one of her chalky hands and pulling her to me before enveloping her in my arms. God, she fits me so perfectly.

I've never been self-conscious of my shorter stature, but I've been told it could possibly be a contributor to my personality, a 'Napoleon Complex' someone once called it. They said my drive, my domineering and aggressive behavior, was an unconscious compensation for my height. I told them to fuck off.

I've dated women in all shapes and heights, ones who towered over me and ones who couldn't even reach my chin wearing heels. I didn't really have a preference. Until now. Vi, who had been stiff when I first pulled her into my embrace, is now completely melted against me, her face going into my neck and breathing me in deeply. When I loosen my arms, she stands back, able to look me in the eye, being as she's only an inch or two shorter than me.

"Are you going to climb?" She glances at the oversized clock on the wall behind the counter. "We still have two hours before closing time."

"Might as well," I reply, swiping the tip of my finger down the bridge of her nose, where she had a streak of chalk. I'm surprised at my own touchy-feely behavior, not usually one for intimate gestures not meant specifically as an act of foreplay, but the pretty blush that fills her cheeks followed by another shy smile makes it worth my confusion.

And the next two hours are filled with these small, stolen touches, becoming an internal game of how many times I can draw out that sweet look on her face.

BEFORE THE lie

BEFORE THE lie

BEFORE THE lie

RE THE lie

lie

Four

Vi

I SLEPT LIKE THE DEAD LAST night, after the excitement of Corbin showing up at the gym unexpectedly. We spent the two hours working mostly on bouldering techniques on the forty-five-degree-angled wall. No ropes or harnesses, just me teaching him different ways to handle a route when gravity was fighting against you. With the pit of regrind beneath us, there was no worry of getting hurt. Just frustration when we'd lose our grip or footing and would fall into the ground-up tires. He had the advantage of massive upper body strength, so he could virtually monkey-bar his way across the wall if he needed to, but that meant he would wear out faster than me, who used less strength and smarter moves to beat a route.

I'd gotten so used to praise for my climbing abilities. I never really knew how to respond to people's admiration, and usually just said thank you and waved off their compliments. But for some reason, under Corbin's impressed and admiring eyes, it meant more to me than anyone else before.

Climbing was always something I did for myself. It made *me* feel good doing something I was talented at. I joined the competitive team, not for the competition itself, but just to test myself. Could I keep up with all of these veteran climbers, who traveled from out of state to gather here and see just who among them were the best of the best? I wasn't in it to win any trophies or titles. I just wanted to see how good at this sport I actually was, seeing how I only did it for fun. When I found out I scored better than my coach, that was pretty mind-boggling. But even that moment didn't compare to the silent but intense way Corbin followed me with his eyes, seemingly spellbound. It also made me feel pretty great knowing that I impressed *him*—a big, strong, badass soldier.

The day has gone by torturously slow. Every time I glance at the clock on the classroom wall, thinking it's almost time for the bell to ring, it's only been a few short minutes. I haven't been able to concentrate worth a crap, but thankfully, being a senior, and with SATs already out of the way, there isn't much to worry about.

Graduation is next month, and it can't come fast enough. I'm going to the community college starting in the fall. I'm not really sure what I want to major in, but I have a lot of time to figure that out while I take care of all my core classes first. I've never really aspired to be anything. When I was little, when people asked me what I wanted to be when I grew up, I always said I wanted to be my mom. To me, nothing could be greater than spending all day taking care of your babies, who love you as much as I love my momma. Being a mom seemed to make her so happy, and that was the most important thing to me—not being rich or famous, or whatever.

Finally, the last bell rings, and I hurry to my locker to grab my stuff before running outside. Mom is usually one of the first cars in the pick-up line, since she knows I like to get to Rock On as early as possible. I hop into her car, throw my bag on the floorboard, and click my seat belt in place, pulling down the visor to look in the mirror.

When I pull my makeup bag out of the front pocket of my backpack, my mom turns to look at me oddly. "What in the world are you doing?" she asks, eyebrows pulled down low.

"What do you mean?" I play dumb, swiping mascara onto my lashes when she stops at a light.

"Why the hell are you putting on makeup when you're about to be at the gym for six hours? Better yet, why are you putting on makeup at all? You never wear makeup. Something that's made your daddy very happy for the past four years." She accelerates gently when the light turns green, allowing me to finish up the other eye before putting the mascara away and grabbing my concealer.

"Nothing. I just... I noticed I looked a little pasty in the bathroom at school today, so I'm just putting on a little something so I don't look sickly," I tell her.

"Uh huh. And it has nothing to do with that adorable little soldier boy who came back to see you yesterday?" She smirks, raising a brow.

"Adorable little soldier boy, Mom? Really? He's a badass Army man," I duck her question.

"He's adorable. I want to put him in my pocket and carry him around with me so I can pull him out every once in a while, to pet his cute little bald head," she says in a baby voice, making my eyes widen in horror. She laughs when she sees my face. "He's twenty, doll. He's almost half the age of your big brother. It's all right if I call him adorable."

"Just swear not to do it to his face," I beg, pinkening my cheekbones with a dab of blush.

"I can't make any promises," she teases, mischief in her bright blue eyes when I glance her way, making me groan.

As she pulls into the gym's lot and parks, I hop out with my bag, but then duck back into the car to hiss, "Behave," when I see Corbin standing propped against his Camaro on the other row of parking spaces.

Mom glances in her rearview mirror at him and grins. "Cute little guy," she says, giggling when my eyes narrow at her before I shut the door, standing up straight to smile at Corbin over the roof of Mom's Cavalier as he approaches.

"You got off early." I smile as he comes around, immediately pulling me into a hug, and I'm instantly filled with the sense of coming home after a long time away. My face automatically goes into the crook of his neck and I breathe him in. His scent is intoxicating. I can tell he's wearing a familiar cologne, but mixed with his chemistry, it's combined to make a unique scent that does *un*familiar things to my body.

"I snuck out. I worked through my lunch hour, so all my shit is done for the day, but I bolted before they could give me anything else to do. But now I'm starving," he adds.

"I only had fries for lunch," I confess, getting pushed away from his body to the sight of his furrowed brows over concerned dark eyes. "I was too excited to see you and it gave me a nervous belly. I could totally eat now, though."

"I could go grab y'all something if you like," Mom offers, having overheard us as she came around the front of her car.

"I'll buy if you fly, ma'am," Corbin tells her, and she smiles at him.

"Deal, but only if you stop calling me ma'am. It's either Eva or Mom, and usually Vi's friends go with the latter." She holds out her hand when he pulls out cash from his wallet. "What do y'all want?"

"Chinese," Corbin replies, at the same time I yip, "Kyoto's!" and we turn to look at each other. I grin as his face softens. "Jinx," he says, his eyes twinkling.

"Not exactly, but I'll still count it," Mom inserts, pulling our attention back to her. "Kyoto's it is. Chicken rice bowl with white sauce for you, doll?"

"Yes, please," I answer, wanting my usual.

"I'll take the same but add beef too, please. And there should be enough there to cover whatever you want too," Corbin tells her, and to my utter dismay, she reaches out and rubs the top of his shiny head.

"See, Vi? Adorable." She winks at me before circling back to get into her car, my mouth hanging open and my cheeks burning as I turn to look at Corbin, who is grinning.

"Your mom thinks I'm adorable," he whispers, as she backs out of her spot.

"I am so freaking sorry. She's getting crazier with age," I breathe, but he chuckles.

"No, this is good. She thinks I'm adorable. Everyone knows the first step is to win over the mother," he tells me, and I tilt my head.

"The first step in what?" I inquire.

"In getting the girl." And with that, he grasps my hand and tugs me toward the entrance of the gym, with me smiling like a fool while trying to hide it with my long hair.

I grab the pen off the desk and sign my name on the clipboard before handing it to Corbin, hurrying off to the bathroom to change out of my school uniform. I shove my clothes into my bag, grabbing my hairbrush out of the front pocket. I pull my hair into its customary high ponytail, taking more time than usual to make sure it's actually straight and smooth on top of my head. "Well, this is about as good as it's gonna get," I tell my reflection, quoting Mia from *The Princess Diaries,* and then I grab my bag and head out the door to put it all in my cubby.

"So what do you want to do first?" I ask Corbin, tying my chalk bag around my hips. When he doesn't answer, I look up at him, and find his eyes narrowed on me. "What?" I grow self-conscious, wondering if I have something hanging out of my nose.

"You look different," he says, taking a step closer.

"Um... I bathed? You haven't seen me not covered in chalk before," I tell him, playing dumb.

He takes another step forward, his head tilted a little, as his eyes burn into me, making me squirm. "You doll yourself up for me, baby girl?" he asks, his voice low.

My eyes widen before I look away, unable to meet his, as I lie, "What? No! You've just never seen me before I start climbing for the day is all."

When I finally look him in those gorgeous chocolaty pools, he smirks. "Okay, Vi," he says softly, "but just for future reference,

I think you're absolutely perfect, covered in chalk, unbathed, messy hair... just the way you are, sweetheart. So in case you ever feel you need to doll yourself up to impress me, just know you don't have to. I'm already impressed."

I feel my face soften, and all I can do is nod.

"But to answer your original question, how about you finally teach me this 'Takeaway' game you told me about?" he suggests, and I jump on it like a lifeline.

"Okay! I love Takeaway!" I grab his arm and drag him over to one of the moderate-level walls, and then pull out my stick of chalk from inside my chalk bag. "So here's what you do. Whoever starts will take their turn making their way across the wall. When they make it to the end, they get to 'take away' one of the rocks by circling it with the chalk. The next person goes, and they aren't allowed to use any of the circled holds. It starts out super easy, but eventually...." I grin, seeing he's got the gist. "If one of the climbers falls, the other climber has to make it in order to be named the winner. If both fall, you each get to try again... *until there is only one*," I say the last part in my best action-movie trailer voice.

He laughs, shaking his head at me. "Sweet. Okay, baby girl. Ladies first." He gestures to the wall and I put the stick of chalk in his hand, turning to start the game.

I make it across in three moves, choosing to use the big, easy jugs while I can. I take the chalk, circling one of the huge handholds in the center, and Corbin takes his place at the start.

I stand back and admire him from behind, loving the way his muscles ripple beneath all those tattoos. I wonder why he's got so many already, seeing as he's only twenty. Did he really get two sleeves and a chest piece all within just two years?

His wife beater fits him like a second skin, showing off the muscles in his back working as he makes his way across the wall. When he finishes and turns to take the chalk from me, he catches me checking out his ass, and my face heats. He doesn't say anything though, just smirks as he chooses the rock he wants to take away.

"Your turn," he tells me, and I swiftly boulder from one end to the other, avoiding the rocks we circled. This time I choose to take away a foothold, bending down almost to the floor to circle one of the rocks. When I turn around to face him, his eyes are on my lower half. I squeak then giggle, swatting at his arm. "What? You're allowed to check out my ass, but I'm not allowed to look at yours?" he teases.

I scoff. "Hey, you checked out mine on day one, thank you very much!"

"Ah, you caught that, did you? I was wondering what you'd tripped over. Guess it was nothing." He chuckles, and I point at the wall.

"Go!" I try to sound stern, but I can't help but laugh.

The game continues, the option of grips and footholds slowly dwindling until there are barely enough to get across. It's Corbin's turn when my mom returns with our food, and she sets it on the picnic table next to the wall we're playing on, sitting down to watch the final couple rounds of our game.

He makes it the two moves to the middle, squatting down low, since we've taken away anything higher, and then leans away from the wall, trying to see where the next handhold is to his right. It's way out of reach, and I smile to myself, realizing he hasn't noticed the mini-jug above, right below the eight-foot bouldering line drawn across the wall, marking the height you're allowed to climb without being on a rope. I don't say anything though. Oh no, I want my bragging rights if I can beat the big, bad soldier.

He readies himself, his muscles bunching, preparing to spring. And when he does, I'm surprised he's able to grasp the rock in his hand, but he misses the foothold and lands on the floor. "Ah shit," he growls, but then laughs, looking up at me. "Your turn, baby girl. I don't see how you're gonna make it though. You're good, but I don't know if you're *that* good. I will bow down if you do."

Won't that be a sight to see, I smirk to myself, reaching into my chalk bag to get a fresh coat on my hands.

I get in the ready position, taking a deep breath, knowing this is the moment of truth. This is the feeling I live for. People underestimate me. They look at me and they just see a slight, plain Jane, thinking nothing of me. This... this is what I love. Getting to show people I'm so much more, at least on the rocks.

I swiftly make it the two moves to the middle, and then rechalk my hands, my heart pounding. But where Corbin had only squatted down enough to bring his body level with grips, I crouch much lower, until my arms are out straight above my head and my ass is nearly on the floor, my feet pressing into the tiny chips screwed into the wall.

"What is she doing?" I hear Corbin mumble to my mom, but I don't hear her answer, tuning everything out but me and the wall.

My eyes glance way up and to the right, seeing the faded olive-green mini-jug I'm aiming for. My heart races as the rest of the world seems to slow down, my focus turning internal, zeroing in on the small but powerful muscles in my legs, the mighty strength in my delicate-looking fingers. *I can do this.*

And with one last pull of air in through my nose, at the moment I force it out through my lips, it seems to send me skyward like a rocket as I lunge for the rock, all of my muscles working together. In one fast, powerful jump up from the low position, I spring like a Jack-in-the-Box as I nail my target, sticking the dyno perfectly with my right hand.

I hear my mom's loud yip along with Corbin's, "What the fuck?!" as my left foot comes to rest on the rock my right hand had left open. I chalk up my left hand before switching my grip on the mini-jug to do the same to my right, and then finish out the route in two more quick moves. I jump from the wall and twirl, my ponytail swinging out from my head and coming to rest on my chest as I land, grinning from ear to ear as I see his shocked face.

Next thing I know, his hard body is pressed to mine as he lifts me in the air, spinning me around and making me laugh. "What the hell was that?" he exclaims. "That was fucking awesome! You gotta teach me! Teach me your ways, great and powerful Spidergirl."

When he sets me on my feet, I take a step back, lift a brow, and point to the ground in front of his rented climbing shoes. "I do believe you said you would bow down if I made it," I say haughtily, but then giggle, not expecting him to actually do it. But to my utter surprise, and Mom's fit of laughter, Corbin drops to his knees, raises his delicious, bulging, tattoo-covered arms above his head, then bows face-to-floor, chanting "We're not worthy," mimicking Garth on *Wayne's World*. It sets off my own full-body laugh, seeing the mostly serious, sinfully sexy man before me being a goofball for once.

When he stands, a heart-stopping smile across his gorgeous face, he brushes his hands together sending chalk into the air. But then suddenly, his eyes narrow, and his smile fades, and I think something is wrong, until...

"Achoo!" He sneezes right as he covers it with his wife beater, the lower half of his face disappearing into the neckline of his shirt.

"Weaksauce. I give it a five out of ten," I say, and then spin on my heel, starting toward the bathrooms to go wash my hands.

Suddenly, Corbin is beside me, and asks, "What is that all about? The scoring thing?"

"Oh, they've done it since before I started coming here. I guess the owner is an atheist or something and got tired of hearing 'bless you' a million times a day, so he started scoring people's sneezes as a joke. I've only been around one perfect ten before. My teammate Joshua came to practice when he had a sinus infection, and when he sneezed, the biggest, greenest snot bubble ballooned out of his nose in front of everybody. It was disgusting and fascinating at the same time," I reply, and he chuckles at my shudder.

We each go into our designated bathroom to wash our hands, and then meet back at the picnic table, where Mom has spread out all our dinner for us. I take a seat on the bench where she's set my bowl of rice covered in hibachi chicken with four lidded containers of white sauce. Corbin sits next to me, and he looks at the thick condiment questioningly as I empty the first one onto my chicken.

"What is that stuff?" he asks, grabbing a fork and tearing it free of the clear plastic wrapper.

"White sauce," I say, licking the remnants from the inside of the little bowl, unconsciously letting out a small moan.

"White sauce?" he repeats, his brow arching and a smirk forming on his lips.

"Mmmmm. Mmm-hmm. I could do shots of this stuff. I think they also call it yum-yum sauce in other places," I tell him, dumping a second container on top of the chicken.

"You'd like shots of yum-yum sauce... in your mouth," he states, and coughs when I nod.

"It's so delicious. Have you never tried it before?" I ask, before licking that one clean too.

"Nope, can't say I've taken white sauce to the face before," he says, his voice tight, as if trying not to laugh.

Suddenly, my hand stops midair as I'm about to dump a third one onto my dinner, and when it clicks in my head why he sounds like that, my face jerks toward him, my mouth and eyes wide open, and my cheeks flaming red. And that's when he and my mother both burst into laughter.

Five

Corbin

THERE IS NOTHING MORE fulfilling than toying with Vi's innocence. Growing up where and the way I did, and then being in the military, around a bunch of testosterone-filled, dirty-minded soldiers 24/7, the sexual innuendos never end. But then there's Vi, so sheltered, so focused on her sport, and her almost anti-social teenaged years, which would normally have been spent with friends and dealing with hormones. She takes everything anyone says at face value. It reminds me of Drax the Destroyer in *Guardians of the Galaxy*, the way he only understands things literally, unable to grasp the concept of metaphors.

But she finally caught on to my gutter-minded references to her yum-yum sauce, and thank God her mom has a great sense of humor, as she damn near fell off her bench, laughing on the other side of the picnic table. And the look on Vi's face—priceless.

We finish eating, and I grab the plastic bag all the food came in and collect our trash, tossing it in the giant trashcan in the very center of the gym. As Eva takes a seat in her usual spot on the couch, Vi gets into starting position on a route she told me she needed to practice, so I plop next to her mom, sending up a huge cloud of chalk and making her laugh.

When it settles, I take a deep breath, calming my nerves so I can do what I told myself I'd do all day at work. No way I'm pussing-out now. *Win the mom, win the girl.* "I have a question for you," I begin, leaning forward and resting my forearms on my knees, clasping my hands together.

"Shoot, honey," she tells me, and gives me her undivided attention.

"Maybe it's old fashioned of me, but as I get to know Vi… she's not like anyone I've ever met before. And I wanted to ask your permission to take her out on a date. I mean, I don't know if her—would you call it *sheltered?*—personality was your parenting style, or if it's just who she is. And I don't mean that in a disrespectful way at all," I add, holding my hand up to assure her. "In fact, I applaud you if it was your doing, because come on. She's eighteen, smart, beautiful, and talented, and somehow hasn't dated in four years."

We both glance over to the wall as we hear Vi hiss, "Shit!" and watch as she stands up from where she fell, brushes off her ass, and then starts at the beginning of the route once again.

"At first, it was a blessing," Eva says quietly. "And Lord knows her father still thinks it is. And in many ways, yes, I still believe it is too. She never stuck with anything when she was younger.

Always so self-conscious. She gave up dancing, because she was too embarrassed to wear the costumes. She gave up piano, because she'd get frustrated when she couldn't follow along with the sheet music the very first time she tried. This is the first and only thing she's put effort into. I think it was because she was naturally gifted in the very beginning, and then she worked at getting even better at it. It wasn't something she initially sucked at, and then had to work hard to *become* talented at it. Call it a character flaw."

She shrugs, and I nod, beginning to understand where she's going with this. "But then she became almost obsessed. Not in a bad way necessarily. I suppose anyone who is really good at something they love could be described as *obsessed*, when they eat, sleep, and breathe that hobby. Yet this isn't a very social sport. Football, basketball, cheerleading... all of those kinds of sports, you're on a team. You have to work together in order to win. This... this, it's just you and the rocks. You shut everything and everyone else out, and you put all of your focus into yourself and keeping your body on the wall, not falling." She looks at me with an almost sad smile.

"I mean, she's on the 'climbing team,'" she continues, gesturing with air quotes. "But really, all they do is warm up and condition together, and then the coach will either teach her a new technique or fix the way a climber is doing something, but there's really nothing social about it."

She sighs. "I guess what I'm trying to say is no, it wasn't me. Yeah, I wanted her in an extracurricular activity to take up some of her time after school to keep her out of trouble, but the way it's taken over her life"—she shakes her head—"that was all her. But to answer your request, yes, *please*, by all means take her on a date. I've never seen her act the way she does around you. She's never really been excited to spend time with another person before. And most importantly, I've never seen her smile so much. You are the only *person* who's ever made her eyes light up the way they do when she beats a hard route." She grins, and it's contagious.

"Wow. That was a lot easier than I thought it would be," I chuckled. "Confession time? I was seriously psyching myself up to asking you all day. I didn't think you'd want your daughter going out with a guy like me." My forearms still resting on my knees, I ungrasp my hands, palms up, and use my eyes to indicate all my tattoos before looking back at her.

"One, you're a Specialist in the army at just twenty years old. That means you don't joke around when it comes to your job. You probably haven't done anything stupid to make you lose rank." She lifts her brows to confirm, and I nod. "Two, the way you were with your lower-ranking soldier. You took great care in making sure he knew y'all were here to have fun. You had him call you by your name, made him your equal for a little while."

One corner of my lips pulls up as that observation reminds me of something. "I had a Master Sergeant once who told me, 'Lowe, when you take off your dog tags at the end of the day, you should take off the soldier mentality along with them.' It kinda just stuck with me, so I try to pass down that bit of advice when I can," I tell her.

"That's very good advice. My husband—Vi's dad—and I have been married since I was 19, many, many moons ago. He's retired Navy. You can still see the military in him, in his neatness and the way he can't stand clutter. The way he eats fast, little things like that. But he was also very good at 'taking off the mentality' as you put it, and I think that's why we've lasted this long," she confides, and it makes me smile.

I really enjoy talking with Eva. She's not like most moms I've met in the past of girls I was interested in. She's never once looked at me disapprovingly, which is a nice change, and she talks to me like the grown man I am, instead of down at me.

"So why is it that you always stay? I see other parents just drop off their kids, much younger than Vi. But you've been here with her all three times I've come. Just curious," I ask.

"Vi's big brother is much older than her. And we tried for a really long time to have another baby, but they just never came. We finally threw in the towel and stopped hoping it was going to work, and since I had some health issues, we didn't feel it was safe for me to do any type of fertility treatments. But then, about three months before Marshall's retirement date from the Navy, lo and behold, I was pregnant. At almost forty years old, with Henry—Vi's brother—about to go to boot camp for the Navy himself, I finally conceived. Not only that, it was a baby girl. I grew up with all brothers, and then I had Henry, so all I wanted in the whole world was a little girl. And there she is," Eva says, holding out her hand toward her gorgeous daughter and smiling, as we hear Vi growl, *"Mother of Gooooooood,"* as she tries desperately to stretch and reach a foothold with her right foot, the tip of her toe barely missing it, with her body turned almost completely sideways on the wall.

"So, one, I just love spending as much time with her as I can get. She was a dream come true for me, and I treat her as the gift she is. There's no way I could just drop her off anywhere and leave her by herself. And two, she's always been so tiny. I mean, look at me." She lifts her arms, indicating how rail-thin she is too. "She takes after me. She can eat a meal the size of a horse—and let me tell you, ever since she started climbing, the girl puts away some damn food with all the energy she burns, so fair warning for your wallet when you take her out. But there isn't anything wrong with her, just a crazy high metabolism. Yet being that little and practically defenseless, I've never been able to let her go off on her own. Because it would be *on her own*. She doesn't really have any girlfriends. The little assholes at school picked on her so bad she never opened up to anyone to make an ally."

"Who the fu—"

"Corbin!" Vi calls, cutting off the fury filling me that someone, anyone, would be giving her shit. "Will you come spot me for a second?" Her voice is strained as she keeps her body flush with the wall.

I jump up and rush to her, shaking off my anger. "What do you want me to do?"

"Just put your hand flat on my back. I've got to see if I'm even tall enough to reach this bitch," she breathes, and I do as she requests, taking some of the strain off her arms as they struggle to keep her close to the rocks.

My hand still pressed there, I take a step back, enough to see if her toe is within reach of the foothold. "You're still about an inch off, baby girl."

"Son of a bitch," she gripes, relaxing into my palm and placing her feet on the ground before standing upright. Her hands shoot to her hips, and I hear her frustrated growl.

I can't help but smile at the pensive look on her face as she tries to figure out how she's going to conquer this route. I have no idea how she'll be able to fix something like not being long enough to reach a rock, but knowing her abilities, I don't doubt she will. She bites her lip as her eyes dart between the holds, and it makes my dick twitch in my shorts.

Not wanting to get a hard-on in basketball shorts in the bright gym, her mom right there watching us, I place my hand on her cheek and turn her to look at me for a moment. "You've got this, baby girl," I tell her, kissing her forehead, and then make my way back to the couch. I sit down gently so I don't send up a chalk cloud, and when I look up at Vi, her wide eyes are on me, mouth slightly open. The look on her face is hard to read, but then she smiles shyly when our eyes meet, and she turns back to the wall.

"Yep," Eva says from beside me, and I look at her. "I'm calling it right now. You're my future son-in-law." She nods once, picks up her book, and flips to her bookmarked page, not saying another word.

As surprising as her words are, what shocks me more is the fact I don't hate the idea. I always told myself I didn't want to be in a relationship, being in the military. Much less married. All you hear are horror stories, soldiers going off to war and receiving Dear John letters, or significant others cheating and rumors getting back through the grapevine.

Nothing good ever comes from being in a serious relationship when you get deployed. Not only all the infidelity bullshit, but also the state of mind it puts you in. When you have someone back home, it can make you depressed and unfocused, so that's why I decided a long time ago that I would be married to my job instead. I haven't had an actual girlfriend since I dropped out of high school and got my GED to go ahead and join the Army.

But after spending the last three days with Vi, and our immediate and unwavering connection....

I sit back, prop my elbow on the arm of the couch, and toy with my bottom lip with the tips of my thumb and pointer finger as I watch Vi work out the route in her head. Then she gets back into starting position once again. This time, when she arrives at the place that's been giving her problems, she doesn't try to reach so far with her foot first. She pulls herself up, both hands on one tiny rock before extending to the next handhold with her right arm. As she grasps it, she's able to swing her entire body to the foothold she had previously been unable to get to, and then completes the route.

Hopping down off the last rock, instead of her customary twirl, she collapses to the ground and sprawls out. I jump up, my heart sinking to my stomach, and run to her, but as I look down, I see her face is covered in a wide grin as her chest pumps with exertion, her arms stretching out above her head. I step over her, putting one foot on the ground on either side of her chest, and cross my arms over mine, glaring down at her. "You just scared the piss out of me," I grumble.

"Sorry," she giggles, her eyes twinkling from the fluorescent light shining down on her from the ceiling.

"I think you should make up for it by going out with me," I state, smirking when her heaving breaths stutter for a moment.

Her eyes widen, her grin relaxes, and she turns her head to glance at her mom, who I see nods her head in approval, before Vi looks back up at me. "O-okay," she replies, and I hold my hand out for her to grasp.

She places her delicate hand in mine, and I pull her up effortlessly to stand, then jerk her forward, wrapping my arm around her lower back to hold her to me. "A kiss to seal the deal?" I prompt jokingly, and she gulps. But to my surprise, she leans up and places a soft, quick kiss to my cheek, and it does more to my heart than the heaviest make-out session I've ever had in my life.

I look over at Eva, with the biggest smile I've had on my face in a long-ass time. "Tomorrow night good, Mom?" I ask her, and lay my cheek against the top of Vi's head as I feel her rest her forehead on my collarbone. The act is so small, but knowing it's Vi—my guarded, innocent, sweet girl, who I now understand doesn't open up to anyone—it makes me feel like the king of the world that she's allowing herself this tiny bit of intimacy.

Voice choked up, Eva replies, "Sounds good to me. Vivian?"

I feel Vi nod against me, and I rub her back gently, hearing her almost purr before she stands to her full height, smiles, and then asks, "So. You ready to climb?"

I chuckle, but allow her to change the subject, knowing I got more out of her than I had expected. "Definitely. How about another game of takeaway? I got to try to win, since you beat me."

And just like that, self-assured Vi returns. "Bring it, soldier boy."

BEFORE THE *lie*
EFORE THE *lie*
BEFORE THE *lie*
RE THE *lie*
lie

Six

Vi

Nervous doesn't even begin to describe what's going on inside me as I wait for Corbin to pick me up. We decided last night on the phone that we'd go see a movie and out to eat. There's not much else to do in our small town next to the base, so we're sticking to the classic first date.

Mom took me shopping this morning, when I started freaking out that all I had were school uniforms and athletic clothes. I think she was more excited than I was for our girly excursion, and ended up buying me way more than just an outfit for tonight. I am now the proud owner of three pairs of skinny jeans, two pairs of denim bellbottoms, about ten new cute tops, and five dresses. Also, a ton of new shoes for every possible occasion, and one thing I've never had a reason to own in my life, but saw and actually drooled over it when we were passing by it in the window, a purse. But not just any purse. It's a lavender solid leather Coach bag that has silver details.

I stroke the leather in my lap as I sit at the small desk in my room before tossing in my lip-gloss, smiling as I remember what Mom said. *"You never ask for anything. You didn't go to prom. I have an envelope tucked away full of money I stashed for things you never ended up wanting to do. If you want the bag, it's yours, doll."* I had squealed and hugged her ferociously before we both danced into the store.

I hear the doorbell ring and glance at the time on my cell—5:42 p.m. He's eighteen minutes early. I'm kind of grateful though. I've been ready for half an hour, and my anxiety has been growing ever since. I toss my bag onto my shoulder, and check myself in the mirror. My white V-cut super-soft T-shirt looks crisp and clean paired with my dark-wash skinny jeans and brown sandals. My long, dark hair is down my back and straightened—something I never take the time to do normally—and it surprises me how long it's gotten, since it usually stays in a bun or ponytail on top of my head. I put on a little blush, some mascara, and lip-gloss, but I don't know how to do much else, so I left it at that instead of attempting and failing anything fancier. With a deep breath in and out, I square my shoulders, feeling more confident in the way I look than I think I have my whole life, and head downstairs.

When I get to the bottom, I see my dad has the door open and is shaking a hand attached to a tattooed wrist, and my heart flips.

"Nice to meet you too, Corbin. My wife speaks very highly of you," Dad says, and opens the door wider, allowing Corbin to step all the way in. When the door shuts, there he is, in all his heart-stopping, drool-inducing glory.

I've never seen him in anything but workout clothes before. Tonight, he's wearing thick-soled brown boots, dark jeans, and a black T-shirt that looks like the seams may burst open it's stretched so tight across his massive biceps. When I look up into his face, he's placing a black ball cap on his head with one hand, and then lifts the other to the bill to squish it, making it frame his forehead. It's a habit I've noticed him do the couple times he's put it on as he leaves the gym.

I smile at him, feeling my face heat as he licks his lips, taking me in much the same way I did him. And we just stand there staring at each other silently until my dad comes back into the foyer, snapping us out of it, when I hadn't even noticed he'd gone outside in the first place.

"All right, Specialist Corbin Lowe, ma man. I took a picture of your license plate, and I now know your full name. If you don't bring my daughter home by a decent hour, I will hunt you down," Dad tells him, clapping Corbin on the shoulder. "Have fun, princess," he directs at me, before heading into the kitchen just as Mom is coming out, wiping her hands on a dishtowel.

"Ignore him, honey," she says, giving Corbin a brief one-armed hug before turning to me. "Oh, Vi, my baby girl. You look beautiful!" She walks over to me, slides open the zipper of my new purse, and I see her tuck a couple of folded bills inside. As she hugs me, she whispers, "A girl should always have cash to get herself home, just in case, baby," before kissing my cheek. "Now y'all have a good time."

I walk over to the open door and feel Corbin's hand come up to rest on my lower back. "Movie starts at 6:30, and we're going to dinner right after. I'll have her back no later than midnight," he tells her, before mouthing to me, *Princess*, and I use the back of my hand to slap him in the gut. Yet I discover there is no gut at all, just rock-hard abs, and he doesn't even flinch, giving me a smirk instead.

"Bye, Mom," I say, and we head out the door. Corbin opens the passenger door of his Camaro for me, and I slide into the black leather bucket seat. As he closes it behind me, I tuck my bag under my legs and put on my seat belt. The interior is completely spotless and empty, except for the small American flag hanging from the rearview mirror.

As he gets in on the driver's side, he starts the car and pulls out of our driveway. Once he's out of my neighborhood and on the main road, he shifts gears and hits the gas, my body suddenly pressing into the seat.

"Like that, do you, baby girl?" he asks, and I realize I have the biggest smile on my face.

"Oh yeah. My brother has a Mustang and takes me on rides when he's home. It's the only time I get to go fast. I'm a roller coaster junkie too," I confess, and laugh as he revs his engine, shifts gears, and speeds through a yellow light.

Soon, though, he slows back down to the speed limit. "As much as I'd like to go all *Fast and Furious* for you, I'd rather not get a speeding ticket on our first date. Your dad would probably never let me have a second one," he says, and I giggle.

"True story."

"Where do you go to ride roller coasters?" he questions, stopping at a red light before turning right.

"I've been to Disney World, Busch Gardens, and King's Dominion, but the closest one is Six Flags. I've been to it several times, since it's only about four hours away."

"I can't remember the last time I went to an amusement park," he confides, and I look over at him with wide eyes.

"Really? Oh, my gosh, we'll have to go soon." The words escape my mouth without thinking, and I feel my face heat. "I mean, if you want to," I add quietly.

He glances at me, hearing the abrupt change in my tone, and reaches over, resting his hot palm on my thigh. "I'd fucking love to take you to ride roller coasters. When we going?"

I grin. "Well, I graduate in about two months. Two weeks before the rest of the school lets out. Probably be a good time to go, before the summer rush. Fewer lines," I suggest.

"Sounds perfect to me, baby girl." He turns up the radio suddenly. "Oh, I love this song. Good shit." I listen to the lyrics, and look at him questioningly before he begins to sing, *"Did you do too many drugs? I did too many drugs. Did you do too many drugs too? Baby."* He tickles my knee on the last drawled out word, making me laugh.

"What the heck is this?" I ask.

"'American Music' by the Violent Femmes," he replies, then taps along as he belts out the rest of the song.

When it ends, I smile over at him. "That must be some kind of California music or something. I've never heard of them before."

"Yeah, I used to smoke weed and listen to them and Pink Floyd all the time back in the day," he says so nonchalantly that my exasperated look catches him off guard. "What?"

"You smoked weed?"

"Who hasn't?" He shrugs, giving me a sexy smirk.

"Um, me. I've never even smoked a cigarette. Much less something illegal."

"Somehow, that doesn't surprise me, baby girl." He squeezes

my leg.

"What's it like?" I ask quietly, turning to face him as much as I can in the bucket seat.

"What, weed? It's really not as big of a deal as people make it out to be. For me, it was just super relaxing. I'd smoke, and then just lie in bed and listen to music. It helped me turn my brain off so I could sleep. I had a lot of bad shit going on around me back then, and it was my escape," he explains.

"What kind of bad shit?" I pry.

He glances over, lifting an eyebrow at me. "Promise not to run?"

Like that would happen, I think. Seeing the kind of man he is now, I'd never hold his past against him. "Promise."

"Well, I told you I was in a gang before I was given the choice of jail or joining the military. But we're not talking about some stupid little no-name group of kids that just call themselves a gang. I was part of one of the big ones out in Cali. I had it tattooed... here," he tells me, pointing at a place on his arm before holding it over for me to see, but all I see is the beautiful Americana sleeve. "Feel it."

I run my fingertips over his bicep, and sure enough, the skin there feels raised in places, as if it's scarred beneath all the ink. "What was it?" I ask, wrapping my hand around his arm as he rests his elbow on the console, proud of myself for bravely keeping up the contact.

"It was the gang's symbols, but in order to join the military, I had to get rid of it. Fastest way to do that, and what many people do, was to take a rock and scrub it out."

"Ouch, didn't that hurt?" I flinch.

"Hell yeah, it hurt, but I wasn't about to waste the money

and take the time to do that laser bullshit. I had a lot of tattoos already by the time I was seventeen, so after it healed, I got it covered up."

"How did you have tattoos already? You have to be eighteen, right?" I probe, feeling like I'm interrogating him, but I can't get enough of how open he's being. He's so interesting, and I want to know everything about him.

"Maybe to get one legally. But I had a buddy who was a tattoo artist, and he did them at his house. I got my first one when I was fifteen. I had all sorts of them by the time I was eighteen. I wasn't happy with the way it was looking, getting patchwork tattoos. I felt like a car with a bunch of mismatched bumper stickers. So when I got here, with one of the best tattoo shops in the US right outside the base's gate, I decided to go in and turn them into sleeves," he explains, and I look down at his arm again.

Sure enough, looking closely, I can see hidden pictures within the overall traditional Americana style artwork. "We'll have to play seek-and-find story time when I can actually see better, instead of in a dark car."

We pull into the parking lot of the movie theater and he chuckles. "I'll tell you all about them, baby girl. Might take a while, because each one has its own meaning. I never got anything that wasn't symbolic to me in some way."

He pulls into a spot and puts the car in park. "What about you? You want any tattoos?" he asks.

"I love tattoos. But as far as I understand, they're really expensive. And since I don't have a job...." I shrug. "No way my parents would give me money for a tattoo. So that will have to wait until I can afford them on my own."

He opens his door and hops out, coming around and opening

mine, where I struggle to get out of the slick and deep leather bucket seat. He holds out his hand to me and chuckles, pulling me up before closing the door. "What are you doing after graduation?" he asks, taking my hand like we've done it every day our whole lives. It's that way for me too. It feels so natural holding hands with him, even though it's something I've never done with anyone before.

"I'm going to the community college in the fall. I was thinking about working at Rock On over the summer during the day. I've actually done that before, worked there during my summer breaks. I mean, I'd be there anyways. Might as well get paid for it too," I reply.

We approach the window of the box office and he buys our two tickets, and I thank him before he takes my hand once again, leading me into the lobby. "What are you going to school for?"

"I don't know yet. I figure I have plenty of time to decide while I get my core classes out of the way first," I admit, as we get in line for the concession counter.

"What, you don't know what you want to be when you grow up?" He smiles.

"No, not really. To be perfectly honest, I've never had any big dreams of becoming something professional. I'm not really good at anything besides climbing. I always just wanted to be my mom." I blush, looking away, embarrassed I don't have a more interesting answer.

"Your mom? Like, you want to be a homemaker?" he asks.

"Yeah. I mean, some people think that's an easy job, but it's really not. It's a lot of work running a household. And she not only keeps it running, but she's amazing at everything that goes into it. We have delicious home-cooked meals every night. She cleans, bakes, grocery shops every week, decorates the house for every season and holiday, all sorts of stuff. And that's with grown children. I can't imagine how busy she was with babies. But she always does everything happily, with a big smile on her face. It all brings her so much joy just taking care of her family."

He tugs on the hand he's holding, bringing my body flush with his, and I lift my eyes to meet his. "There is nothing to be ashamed of about wanting to be a homemaker. Look at *you*, and from the little bit I've heard you two say about your brother, it sounds like he turned out great as well. Maybe if I'd had that, I wouldn't have been such a little shithead when I was younger. That's a very admirable job, Vi," he assures me, and I melt against him. "I just don't see how you planned on seeing that dream out, keeping to yourself and never dating." He chuckles, winking at me.

"No one ever made me stop and take a second look before you," I breathe, getting lost in his amazing dark chocolate eyes.

He smiles, and his eyes lower to my mouth when I unconsciously bite my bottom lip. The next thing I know, his soft, full lips are against mine, and a jolt runs through my whole body. As his hand comes up to rest against the side of my neck and I feel him trace my jawline with his thumb, everything and everyone begin to disappear.

The bright lights and menu above the concession stand are the first to dim, as I take in the heat of his body pressed to mine. The sound of the popping machine and the people talking around us in line are the next to fade, as I enjoy Corbin's steady inhale and exhale through his nose, and then the barely audible growl he lets loose as he wraps his arm around my lower back. Finally, the strong smell of buttery popcorn and sugary sweet candy in the air dissolves, as all I breathe in is the delicious and intoxicating scent of the man before me.

The entire world has completely evaporated as time stands still, and all that's left are the two of us in our sweet embrace. It's not an inappropriate public display of affection, nothing overly passionate for anyone around us to lewdly observe, but heart-stopping just the same. And it seems to end just as quickly as it began when Corbin gently pulls away.

I blink up at him. "I thought the first kiss normally comes at the end of the date," I whisper.

His face serious, he presses his forehead to mine, and replies, "You'll learn not much about me is normal. I just hope none of it scares you away."

I smile, trying to brighten his suddenly somber tone. "Maybe if we mix your un-normalness with my boringness, we'll even each other out."

"Vi, there is nothing boring about you, baby girl. You just needed someone to bring you out of your shell," he says, tucking my hair behind my ear.

"Are you calling me a hermit crab?" I giggle, as we make our way to the front of the line.

"Hottest hermit crab I've ever seen." He chuckles, and looks up at the menu board. "Do you know what you want?"

"Chocolate-covered almonds and Sprite, please," I answer, a little stunned. No one's ever called me hot before, at least not right to my face like that.

"Chocolate-covered almonds, a large Sprite, and a large popcorn please," Corbin orders, and pulls out his wallet to pay.

"Ew, popcorn is gross," I mumble teasingly.

He gives me a horrified look. "What? I don't know if this is going to work. Who doesn't like popcorn?"

I laugh, smacking his arm. "Again, me, that's who. It always gets stuck in my teeth."

We grab our snacks, and then find two seats in the back of the theater, where he places the giant drink in the cup holder between us.

"You said you didn't have what I do. So what *did* you have, if your mom wasn't home with you like mine?" I ask curiously.

"My mom and dad divorced when I was little, and I lived with my mom in California, while my dad lived in the Midwest. She had an office job that paid really well, but it had long hours. She didn't like leaving me alone, so I had a babysitter that would come over and hang out with me until bedtime, and then Mom would get home sometime after that. It was all well and good until I got a new babysitter when I was fourteen, and I was kind of pissed that she still thought I needed to be looked after. I mean, I was fourteen, not a child anymore. But then the babysitter showed up, an eighteen-year-old college student, and that was the end of my bitching," he tells me, and a feeling I can only describe as jealousy fills me.

"Pray tell," I prompt, because apparently I want to torture myself.

"Well, she was this hot older chick, and although I was only fourteen, I've always looked older. I took wrestling in school, and was a third degree black belt in Kenpō, so I had quite the body, even back then. I lost my virginity to her soon after—"

"Your eighteen-year-old babysitter slept with a fourteen-year-old?" I gasp, completely flabbergasted. "Isn't that illegal? Plus, um… she was in college, you said. So why the hell would she want to sleep with a kid when she had people her own age?"

"One, it's only illegal if you get caught, and two, I didn't look much younger than I do now, so I'm sure she wasn't thinking about my age at the time. We were just two people alone in my house who knew my mom wouldn't be home until late," he explains.

I look at him, imagining myself in his babysitter's position if I would've cared how old he was, and I guess I can see why it didn't matter to her. He's freakin' perfect. "I suppose."

"But it all went downhill from there. She's the one who introduced me to drugs. It started out as just weed, but then she started bringing over things like Ecstasy and all sorts of shit. She snuck me out to a party, and introduced me to her friends who were in the gang, and one thing led to another." He takes a sip of drink before eating a handful of popcorn.

"And your mom had no idea?" I ask.

"Nope, not until I was sixteen and she happened to see one of my tattoos. But by then, I was already so submersed into all the bad shit that I didn't really care about her feelings. Maybe if she'd caught me before then.... But I don't waste time on 'what ifs'. Because if my life hadn't been that way, I would never have joined the military and I wouldn't be the person I am today. It's not my mom's fault. I don't blame her for never noticing. She was just a trusting person who believed her son when I told her I really liked my babysitter and how all we did was my homework and watch TV until I went to bed. Also in her defense, I got really good at lying and hiding shit. A person becomes very crafty when they become an addict."

Just then the lights lower in the theater, effectively cutting off our conversation. I open my box of candy, and pop two in my mouth. As we watch the previews, I glance over at Corbin, the lights and shadows playing over his handsome features, and I can't help but think how grateful I am that his babysitter was such a bad influence, because I probably wouldn't have met him otherwise. I reach over and grab a handful of his popcorn, not being able to resist the smell any longer, and toss it in my mouth.

He looks over at me, eyebrows furrowed. "I thought popcorn was gross?"

"But it just smells so good. I can't stand the way it makes my teeth feel though," I tell him, swiping my tongue across my teeth, unintentionally drawing his eyes to my mouth. "Plus, it tastes really good when you mix the salty popcorn with the sweet chocolate."

"Really? Let me see," he whispers, and moves forward to kiss me, but before his tongue can dip into my mouth, my head jerks back as an explosion goes off on the big screen, startling me as the surround sound makes it seem like we're under attack. Seeing that it's just part of the trailer for an upcoming action movie, I giggle and shake my head.

"Here," I murmur, and pour out a couple of my chocolate-covered almonds into my hand before holding them out to him. But instead of letting me drop them into his hand, he dips his face and eats them directly out from between my fingers, the feel of his lips on my sensitive fingertips sending a surge of tingles to my core.

I watch as he eats another handful of popcorn, his face becoming thoughtful. He leans toward me to whisper in my ear, "You're right. That's delicious, but I would've rather tasted it on you."

My face falls, but I try to be as open as he's been with me. "I... I've never done that before, Corbin." He pulls back and looks me in the eye, but my gaze drops to his chest. "Just... don't get frustrated with me, okay? I know I'm not some super cool chick who has all this experience that'll rock your world like your babysitter did. So just please... try not to get mad at me when I don't know how to do something, all right?"

Suddenly, the drink is removed and the armrest is lifted from between us. He sets his popcorn in the chair next to him, and next thing I know, I'm in Corbin's lap and he's cradling my face with his hand.

"One thing I can promise you, Vi. I will never get frustrated or be mad at your innocence. We will take this thing as slow as you need. I'm normally not a patient man, but if it means getting to taste you and have you all to myself, I'd wait forever," he says so sincerely I feel tears prickle the backs of my eyes. He pulls my face down to his for a soft, tender kiss, and then he lifts me back into my seat, grabs his bag of popcorn, placing it between his knees, and turns his attention back to the screen. I blink a few times, wondering how the hell I'd gotten so lucky to find someone who actually *gets* me. And with that thought in mind, I bravely reach over with my right hand and lace my fingers with his left, feeling his grip tighten as he rests our joined hands on his thigh.

After I finish up my candy, I spend the last thirty minutes with my head on Corbin's shoulder, feeling more at peace snuggled against him than I ever have.

Corbin

MY ASS IS COMPLETELY numb, my arm is asleep, and I'm pretty sure my fingers are about to fall off from lack of circulation, but I'll be damned if I move even a centimeter. I don't want to risk Vi's head leaving my shoulder or her hand pulling out of mine. Especially since she's the one who initiated both.

I've never been one for holding hands, and I damn sure haven't ever been known for being a cuddler. But having Vi so close, snuggled into my side, her tiny body fitting against mine so perfectly, I could sit here forever.

But the movie ends, and as soon as the credits start rolling, Vi lifts her head and reaches across me for the drink, and I feel the loss like she's cut off one of my limbs.

"I'm starving. Where we going for dinner?" she asks, standing up and stretching her arms above her head, which lifts her shirt and bares a sliver of the perfect, creamy skin of her stomach, making me instantly hard.

I exhale slowly and stand, waiting to adjust myself until she turns away from me to lead the way out of our row of seats. "How about Olive Garden? It's just right up the street," I suggest.

"Ooh, sounds good," she replies, holding the railing to make her way down the steps ahead of me.

"I love their breadsticks," I say, watching her ass sway with her every step.

"Psh. No. If it's breadsticks you want, then you need to try Fazoli's."

"No way. No one has better bread sticks than Olive Garden." I shake my head.

She turns around on the bottom step to face me, looking up at me with a challenge in her eyes. My dick throbs behind my waistband, where I've got it tucked. "Trust me. Fazoli's has the most delicious, hot, buttery, garlicky breadsticks ever. Olive Garden's don't hold a candle."

"Wanna make a bet?" I ask, a smirk pulling up my lips.

She straightens and tosses her hair over her shoulder. "What kind of bet?"

"I don't know yet. Let me think about it on our way there."

As I get into the driver's seat of my Camaro after closing Vi's door, I realize something. "Vi, I noticed your mom's car in your driveway, and what I assumed was your dad's truck, but no other vehicle. Do you not have a car?"

"Why have a car if I don't have a license?" She shrugs.

"You don't have your driver's license?" I ask, my face obviously showing my shock, because she giggles and touches the crease between my eyebrows. "But you're eighteen."

"I mean, I went through Driver's Ed and got my permit and stuff, but driving terrifies me. The thought of having to be in control of anything, even a vehicle...." She shakes her head. "In my class, I was okay, because my teacher had his own set of pedals and a steering wheel on his side of the car, so I knew if I were to screw up, he could take over and get us out of danger. But in a normal car.... Scares the shit out of me."

I try to ignore the images that her hating to be in control of anything brings to mind, and I refrain from telling her I'd happily take control of whatever she'd like. But her being too scared to drive pushes past all that. "Baby girl, you need to get your license. You don't want to be dependent on everyone else to get you anywhere you need to go. It's just lack of confidence.

I think with enough practice, your fear of driving would lessen."

"I don't really need it though. I only go to school and to Rock On. Plus, cars and insurance and all that is expensive," she justifies.

"Yeah, but soon, you'll be going to college, and then working at the gym. You don't want your mom to have to keep taking you everywhere, do you?" I ask gently.

"I guess not. I haven't really thought about it," she replies honestly, wringing her hands in her lap.

"I've got it." I reach over and place my hand between hers, lacing my fingers through hers to stop her nervous fidgeting. "If I don't like Fazoli's breadsticks better than Olive Garden's, then you have to practice driving with me. If I do, then you don't have to."

"That's not fair," she whines. "You'll say you don't like their breadsticks better just to make me drive."

I smirk. "That's true, even though I doubt anyone is going to be able to top my love of Olive Garden's breadsticks. I mean, come on. Their initials are OG. They're the OG of Italian food, straight up gangsta," I reply, gaining the laugh I was hoping for. "Then just let me teach you to drive. I promise I won't let anything happen to you."

She lets out a growl of frustration, looks over at me with the most adorable scowl I've ever seen, and then looks down. "Oh hell no! You have a stick shift. No way," she says, shaking her head.

"I'll take you in your mom's car then. It's an automatic, right?" I prompt, knowing her mom has a little four-cylinder Chevy Cavalier.

"Ugh. Fine. If you can convince my mother—the woman who

won't let anyone drive her car—to let you take me to practice driving, then yes, Corbin. I'll learn," she says with such self-assurance that it makes me believe there's no way in hell I'll be able to talk her mom into letting me use her car. But after our conversation at the gym, I'm confident I'll be able to sweet-talk Eva out of her keys.

"Deal. Now where is this place? I'm hungry."

"Would you like another breadstick?" the waitress asks, the wicker basket full of the carb-loaded little pieces of heaven hanging on her arm, her tongs at the ready to give me another two after the dozen I've already eaten.

"Last round and that's it for me. I'm stuffed," I reply, looking over at Vi, her expression of triumph still in place since my first bite of the best damn breadsticks I've ever tasted in my life. The waitress leaves, and I lean forward so only Vi can hear me. "If you don't wipe that smirk off your face, baby girl, I'm going to bend you over my lap and spank your sexy little ass."

Her jaw drops and her cheeks turn an attractive shade of pink in the dimly lit restaurant. Her eyes dart to the couple at the next table over, and she leans forward, over her plate of half-eaten spaghetti. "I'd like to see you try, soldier. I've never been spanked in my life," she tells me haughtily, and my dick instantly hardens. She's grown bolder over dinner, talking to me openly as she's answered every question I've asked about herself. I think it's because I've been open and honest with her as well, sharing everything about my past without trying to hide anything.

"It won't happen the first time I make you mine, Vi, but you can bet that sweet ass I'll be turning it red someday soon."

Her mouth opens and closes like a fish before she sits back in her seat and takes a sip of her drink. "I skipped a night of climbing to get threatened with spankings," she pouts.

"Trust me. When it happens, you'll be begging for more. And by that time, rocks will no longer be your favorite thing to climb," I assure her, and sit back to watch what I said click into place. Yup, there it goes. And as usual, when one of my sexual innuendos finally meets its mark in her mind, her eyes widen, her face pinkens, and her mouth falls open once more. One of my favorite expressions I can get her to make.

She clears her throat and tries to change the subject, but I'm having too much fun making her squirm to let her escape my dirty mind. "What's your favorite movie?" she asks.

"*Harry Potter*. And after we watch it, I'll *avada kedavra* that pussy," I reply, and she gasps.

"You did not just say you'd use the death spell on my *lady bits,*" she hisses the last bit, and I can't help but chuckle.

"What's yours?" I counter, taking a bite of my fresh breadstick, which I begrudgingly admitted were the best ones I'd ever eaten as soon as I took a bite of the first one that came with my chicken fettuccini alfredo.

"*My Big Fat Greek Wedding*," she answers, and I nod.

"Love that movie. I have it on DVD."

"Really?" Her eyes brighten. "Okay, you win some cool points back. What's your favorite color?"

"Pink... like your pu—"

"Corbin!" she cuts me off, covering her eyes with her hands. "I know pink is not your favorite color, dammit."

I throw my head back and laugh, and when I look at her once again, she's uncovered her eyes and is watching me with a sweet smile on her face, as if she's enjoying my laughter. "Orange. My favorite color is orange."

"Seriously? I don't think I've ever heard anyone say orange is their favorite before." She tilts her head to the side.

"It's a bright, happy color. I've just always liked it for some reason. I bet I can guess yours," I say, and she sits up straight.

"Shoot."

"Purple."

"How'd you know?" she questions, her brows lowering but a smile on her lips.

"Your harness and your bag. The harness is important to you, a piece of crucial gear for your favorite activity, and it has purple details. Your bag isn't a cheap one. So one would assume you wouldn't get it in a color that isn't one you really love."

"Nice. Yes, purple is my favorite. I'd wear a lot more of it if I didn't have a school uniform. My whole room is done in different shades," she tells me.

"Even your bed?" I ask, an evil little grin spreading across my face.

"Yeees, even my bed." She rolls her eyes.

"Ah, so now I can better picture you when I'm lying in my bed talking to you on the phone every night."

Her smile returns. "What does yours look like?"

"I'll show you mine if you show me yours, baby girl," I tease, laughing at how easy it is to make her squirm. When she growls, I give in. "Okay, okay. Mine has an outdoor scene on it. It's a buck in the middle of the woods. I have a thing for stuff like that, and Native American artwork. I'm half Cherokee, and I love hunting, so it fits me."

"Cherokee. That must be where you get your gorgeous dark eyes from. Which half?" she asks, and my chest puffs up a little that she likes my eyes. Even though I've heard it countless times before, it actually means something coming from her.

"My dad's side. My mom is Irish." I glance down at my G-Shock watch, seeing it's only 9:38 p.m. "Well we have lots of time before I promised to have you home. Anything you want to go do?"

"I can't think of anything. I'm usually in bed by now, right after getting home from climbing," she replies with a shrug.

"I could take you to an empty parking lot and teach you how to drive stick," I suggest.

"Hell no," she squeaks, but then looks at me with a straight face. "If you promise not to bug me about learning manual transmission, I'll seriously consider saying yes to the driving practices in my mom's car. I'm sure if I asked her nicely, she'd say yes. Especially if you were the one going with me and not her."

"Deal. I had already planned on sweet talking her into it anyways." I grin, and she throws her napkin at me. "When's your birthday?" I inquire.

"September 3rd. Yours?"

"August 26th."

"You'll be 21, yeah?" she confirms, and I nod. "What do you want to do for your birthday? Any big plans to go out and get white girl wasted?"

"Nah, I don't drink anymore. Did enough of that when I was way younger. Doesn't seem like it'll be very cool after I can do it legally," I joke.

"Really? I've never heard of anyone not wanting to drink on their twenty-first birthday."

"Confession time?" I wait for her nod. "I had a pretty fucking tragic experience when I was a teenager that turned me off drinking for the rest of my life." I shift in my seat, clearing my throat. I've never told anyone this story before, because I try not to ever think about it. "I had a girlfriend. She was a total sweetheart. She was the only person who ever got me to pay attention to anything besides the gang I was in. One night, there was a little fair in town, and we used our fake IDs to drink while we were there. We went on all the rides, the typical shit, like The Zipper and Rock-n-Roll Express, all those spinny type of rides. We went back to her house, where I spent the night. Her parents weren't home. We passed out, totally drunk, and exhausted from all the fun we had at the fair. And when I woke up the next morning... well, she didn't."

Vi gasps, covering her mouth. "Oh my God, Corbin. What happened?"

"She had vomited in her sleep and suffocated. We were so drunk that her throwing up didn't wake either of us up. The only thing I can be grateful for was she didn't suffer. She died in her sleep. That day, I swore I would never drink again. If not for myself, then for the safety of my friends. I'll stay sober to take care of them, so if that ever happens to any of them, I'll be there to wake them up."

"I'm so sorry," she tells me quietly. After a beat, she offers me a bit about herself. "My parents don't drink. My dad was a sailor for twenty-two years and never drank a sip of anything other than wine at church every Sunday. We've never had it in our house, so I've never had a drink before. Add that to the long list of things I've never done."

"Trust me, it ain't all that great. Now weed, on the other hand. That's a whole different story." I grin, trying to get back to the jovial conversation we had before.

"I'll take your word for it." She smiles. "You ready to go?" she asks, scooting back from the table.

"Ready to go, but not ready to leave you. We'll figure it out." I stand and take her hand in a loose hold, running my thumb across her palm. I discovered, while sitting in the theater and holding her hand, that though small and delicate, she has some pretty impressive callouses across the top of her palm, right below the webs of her fingers. I actually love that she has that tiny bit of toughness to an otherwise soft and fragile exterior. It's much like her interior as well. She's innocent and sweet, but God knows the walls she's built around herself are as strong as a fortress.

The dynamic between us is completely opposite of what I'm used to. It's usually me hiding, closing myself off, not letting anyone know the real me. It's always the other person trying to pry bits and pieces of my true self out of me. But for some reason, with Vi, I'm an open book. I spill everything freely. All she has to do is ask, and the truth is hers for the taking. And it's been so long since I've given a shit about another person enough to want to get to know them that me pulling answers from Vi feels like a new experience in itself. But it's a challenge I readily accept. With her, I can't just order her to tell me things or do something, like I would with one of my soldiers. I have to treat her equal to me. Give and take. It's confusing the fuck out of the Dominant part of me, but oddly exciting to the man.

"Is there a park around here somewhere?" I ask, making a

left onto the main road that leads to her neighborhood.

"A park? It's probably closed this late, but yeah. Right up here," she tells me, pointing me in the right direction. We pass the fire station, and behind it, I see a couple of baseball fields, a basketball court, and finally an open area with a playground, a large swing set, and a merry-go-round.

I pull into the parking lot and turn off the ignition. There isn't much light out here, just a couple of floodlights that illuminate a piece of the playground and one of the baseball fields.

"It's closed, Corbin. That sign when we entered said park hours were from 5:00 a.m. to 7:00 p.m. It's almost ten," Vi says, looking around the abandoned area.

"Is there a locked gate keeping us out, baby girl?" I prompt, and she looks over at me, brows furrowed.

"Clearly, there's not a fence around it," she replies, gesturing out the windshield.

"Then it's all good. Live a little," I tease, unbuckling both our seatbelts. "If a cop shows up, we just didn't notice the sign when we came in, and we go on our merry way." I open my door and hop out, going around the car. I literally have to drag her out of the vehicle, but as soon as she's in a standing position, I reach beneath the backs of her thighs and swiftly lift her into my arms, and she immediately stops her playful struggle. Her arms come up to lock around my neck, and she melts against me. It's a curiously abrupt change in her demeanor, but I'll take it nonetheless.

I kick her door closed and carry her over to the merry-go-round, sitting down on the edge with her in my lap, and it brings me back to the movie theater, when I'd pulled her into my lap to assure her I wouldn't get upset with her inexperience. There's something about this position, her small body cocooned within the strength of my arms, that puts her completely at ease, the most relaxed and at peace I've ever seen my beautiful Vi. The ever-present worried look in her eyes, which is only ever replaced by an expression of complete concentration when she's climbing, disappears, and words can't describe what it does to me that I can give her that sense of comfort just by holding her.

She sinks against me, her head resting on my shoulder, the heat of her pressed against my chest soothing something inside me I didn't know was there. Suddenly, it isn't thoughts of dominating her, teaching her the things *I* needed to satisfy my urges that play on repeat inside my mind. No. Instead, in their place is an overwhelming need to protect her, to remove the weight of the walls she's built around herself and place them on my shoulders, just so she won't have to bear the weight on her own. For the first time in my life, I want to be someone's savior; I want to be the person *she* turns to, to make things better for *her*, without anything in return but the satisfaction that I made everything all right in her world.

It's a strange feeling, because God knows I'm a selfish bastard. It's why I get uncomfortable when random people tell me, "Thank you for your service." They thank me like I do my job for them, when really, I do it for myself, for my family, for *our* freedom.

But Vi brings out a facet of myself I didn't know existed, one that is a fierce protector who wants to snap and snarl at anything that would dare do anything to harm what's mine.

Mine, it growls, as I turn my face and bury my nose at the top of her head, inhaling the scent there.

"Is it always this way?" she asks suddenly, and I feel her arms come loose from around my neck, but her fingers begin to play at the back of my head, lightly stroking along the stubbly hair that's probably tickling her fingertips.

Such a vague question, but somehow, I know exactly what she means. "No, baby girl. It's never been this way for me before," I confess, laying my cheek on top of her head.

"It's like I've known you forever. You don't feel like a stranger—well, not a *stranger*, but someone pretty new—to me. Almost like I might've known you in another life or something. Does that sound weird?" She tilts her head back and I lift mine, looking down into her gorgeous green eyes, which are imploring me to soothe away her doubts.

"Before I met you, I would've said yes, because I wouldn't have understood what you're feeling. But, Vi, it's the same one I'm having right now. I know exactly what you mean. And as weird as it may be to someone who hasn't felt it before, how scary it is to be falling for someone so quickly"—I shake my head—"I'm not going to fight it. It was fighting and stupid shit that landed me in juvie. I fight every day in the military. When I get deployed, it's a war over there too. But you? I'll fight *for* you, but that's the only battle you ever have to worry about when it comes to us."

She blinks up at me, a sweet smile lifting the corners of her lips. "So what does that make us?"

"It makes you mine. And I'm yours, baby girl," I whisper, bending down to kiss her softly.

"Does that mean I'm your girlfriend?" she breathes against my lips.

I lift my hand to her jaw then slide it down to let it rest against her sternum, watching as she closes her eyes and presses herself into my palm, seemingly unaware that she's doing it. My cock hardens painfully behind the zipper of my jeans, and she must feel it, because she squirms in my lap.

A growl escapes me before I can stop it, and my nostrils flare, but when I get myself under control, forcing myself not to spin around, lay her flat in the middle of the merry-go-round, and take her right here in this empty park, my voice is steady. "You're so much more to me than what that word implies. But for all intents and purposes, yes. I'm not even going to ask, because you have no choice." I grin, so it seems like I'm joking, but I'm really not. I wasn't kidding when I told her I'd fight for her, and I wouldn't take no for an answer.

Thankfully, this isn't a battle I have to worry about, because her face alights with the most beautiful smile I've ever seen and she laughs before nodding. "Fair enough," she says, and lifts her chin for another kiss. I give her what she wants, but when I try to deepen the kiss, tracing my tongue along the seam of her lips, she ducks her head, burying her face in my neck.

"Don't run away, little mouse," I murmur against her ear, and she nuzzles further into me. "What are you afraid of?"

"That I'll be terrible at it," she replies softly.

"And if you are, I'll teach you, and we can practice all you want until you get it just right," I rumble, feeling her shake her head in the crook of my neck.

"Is this your character flaw coming out to play?" I ask.

"Huh?" Her hot breath puffs against my flesh.

"Your mom told me you don't like to try anything new because you're afraid to fail right off the bat. You won't allow yourself to even attempt something, not knowing whether you'll be a pro at it from the start or not," I tell her, and she mumbles under her breath, *"I'm gonna kill her."*

"It's okay, Vi. No one's going to laugh at you. No one is going to make fun of you. I'm sure as hell not, and I'm the only one you're going to be kissing. So let me teach you," I implore, my hand moving around to the back of her neck then up into her hair before fisting it between my fingers. I use my grip to gently tug her head back, forcing her to look up at me instead of allowing her to hide any longer. "Can I teach you?"

She doesn't reply, but her chest rises and falls rapidly with every panted breath she takes. I lower my mouth to just above hers and hover there, the tension building as the seconds tick by without her answer. I tell myself I will not do it without her permission. I will give her sweet pecks pressed to her lips, and that's it, until she actually tells me she's ready to go any further.

She still doesn't say anything, so I decide to make a confession, hoping to shock her into answering. "You know, that's my favorite part about you. Physically, that is. You couldn't stop me, even if you wanted to. I could control you," I whisper slowly, allowing every ounce of my desire for her to fill my voice.

She gulps, and her perfectly white two front teeth clamp down on that luscious, pouty bottom lip of hers, making my cock throb beneath her ass. I feel her tremble, and it takes everything in me not to say fuck it and show her exactly what I want to do to her without waiting for her consent. Yet, I wait, showing more self-control than I ever thought possible.

"I *could*," I repeat, "but... I want you to want me bad enough to ask for it. I won't make you beg for me. At least not yet." I do nothing to hide the mischievous glint in my eyes as I stare down into hers, which I see are glazed with want, but still enough fear that she just... won't... answer.

Suddenly, she stands, and I release my grip on her hair before

I accidentally hurt her. I watch as she flees, but she doesn't go far. Just to the swing set on the other side of the playground, where she picks the one directly in the center and sits, using her feet to walk herself as far back as the chains allow before lifting her legs in the air. I watch her swing herself for a few moments, letting her have her space.

When she comes to a stop, she clasps her hands together, her arms circling the outside of the chains, and she leans way back, looking up into the cloudless sky. I stand and make my way over to her, sitting down in the swing next to hers, and mimic her position.

We're quiet for a long time, just enjoying the silence. It's not an uncomfortable silence, which is surprising, seeing how she just ran from me. But eventually, I speak up, if nothing but to get to know her more by opening up myself. "When I first moved here, the first thing I noticed was all the stars. We arrived in the middle of the night, and as soon as I stepped off the bus, I looked up, and the whole sky was filled with them. In the city I'm from in California, there's so much smog you can't see the stars." I look over at her and see her eyes are on me instead of the sky. "I mean, you can see a few of the brightest ones, but nothing like this."

"I guess since I grew up here and they've always been there, I never take the time to appreciate them," she murmurs, glancing up once more. "That, and I don't spend a lot of time outside."

"You don't go real rock climbing?" I ask.

"I've never been, no." She shakes her head.

"Isn't that the point of climbing in a gym, to learn so you can eventually go climb a mountain or something?"

"Not for me. I really have no desire to outdoor climb. The

thought actually scares me," she admits.

I spin my swing around to face her, the chains crossing in front of me. "Have you ever considered, baby girl, that what you think you're feeling as fear is actually just excitement? Adrenaline?"

She looks at me, her eyebrows lowering. "What do you mean?"

"I'm seeing a pattern with you. You think you fear trying new things, when in all actuality it's probably the same feeling everyone gets before they take a leap of faith. I get that feeling every time I try something I've never done before. Learning to rappel, the first time I shot my rifle, the first time I jumped out of an airplane. But now, it's like a habit. Where most people would take that leap, no matter how small, knowing it's a learning experience, you just can't seem to make yourself jump. Is it all a fear of failure, or is it something else?" I press quietly.

"You jump out of airplanes?" she asks, instead of answering, and I sigh, shaking my head.

"Yeah, Vi. I jump out of airplanes. I'm a paratrooper," I mumble.

"I thought you were a sniper." She tilts her head.

"You really know nothing about the Army, do you?" I ask, chuckling, and she shakes her head. "I'm in an airborne infantry division, which means I'm a paratrooper. I jump out of airplanes to get into otherwise denied areas during an operation. Then, once I'm in, I'm a sniper. I don't run in guns ablazin'. Alone, with a partner, or with a small team, we set ourselves up in a concealed position. Our slogan is *One Shot One Kill*. Only the best marksmen can have my job. I'm highly trained in many more areas than the regular Joe. I've always been good at shooting, ever since I was a kid and my dad took me hunting, but it wasn't until I was in the Army that I learned just how good I could be.

All that bullshit my teachers used to tell me in school about if I just applied myself, I could do great things... I finally did that once I saw what a natural talent I had at making a bullet hit its target. Every. Single. Time."

"That was me with climbing. Once I saw I had a natural gift for it, that's when I really got into it. It was the trying it for the first time that was the hard part," she confides, and then softly, she asks, "Have you... have you ever had to shoot anyone?"

I look her in the eyes. "No. Not yet. I've never been deployed. But when I go, I will. It's my job. It's what I've been trained to do. Do I feel what you're feeling every time you're faced with something you've never tried before? You bet. Anxiety, excitement, and maybe a little bit of actual fear. But I know when I get over there, it'll be either kill or be killed. If I don't do my job to the best of my ability, I won't make it home. So I have to suck up those feelings, store them away, and do what I'm over there to do."

Finally, I'm rewarded for my complete honesty, because she opens up at last. "Apparently, I'm an easy target," she whispers, looking down into her lap. "For some reason, bullies single me out the minute they meet me, and they're ruthless. I hate confrontation. When someone picks on me, I seize up. I think I might've been a possum in another life, because when confronted, I basically play dead. Words won't come out. My brain doesn't make up any witty comebacks in my defense. Nothing. I freeze. I can't even run away from it. I just have to stand there and take their wrath. Cruelty I did nothing to deserve."

A single tear slides down her cheek, and I see red, wanting to tear apart every asshole who's ever said an unkind word to this amazing girl before me. But I swallow it back, wanting to hear what she has to say. "What could they possibly pick on you for?" I murmur, trying to keep the growl out of my voice.

She scoffs. "It would be easier to name the things they don't tease." She wipes at her face with the back of her hand then grips the chain of her swing once again. "I'm skinny. Always have been, and looking at my mom, I probably always will be. No matter how much I eat. So they spread rumors I was anorexic. The one time I tried to defend myself, pointing out how much I eat, for everyone to see right there in the lunchroom at school, they said I must be bulimic then. 'Don't sit near Vi. She probably smells like barf, since she throws up her food.'"

She sniffs, and the sound breaks my heart. "When all the other girls my age started hitting puberty and growing boobs, mine never came. I got a poem in my locker disguised as a love letter one day. I had been so happy that a boy was actually nice to me. I had a secret admirer? Like... you have no idea how absolutely thrilled I was someone had written me a note. I didn't even care who it might've been from. Sad, I know. But then I opened it up, and it wasn't very loving at all. 'Roses are red. Violets are black. Why is your chest as flat as your back?'"

She laughs, but it's not a happy sound. "To make it worse, the boys who had sent it to me were standing across the hall watching me while I read it. And when they saw how much it hurt me, did they apologize? Hell no. They pointed and laughed at me, then snatched the paper out of my hand to gloat to anyone who walked by. So proud of themselves."

She shakes her head and looks up at me, her eyes brimming with tears. "You know, I was actually pretty good at dancing. I had been doing it for several years. Tap, ballet, and jazz classes twice a week. I grew up with a lot of the kids. No one in the class was from my school, so it was my escape, to be around people my age who weren't complete jerks to me. I loved it there." She looks back down into her lap. "But then these new kids signed up. A set of twins, a boy and a girl. They were really good, having moved here from another state, where they danced since they were little too. The girl was really nice, but the boy... it's like he had that same radar in him, the one that singled me out as an easy target. Not only did he pick on me for the usual—how skinny I was, how flat-chested—but he also went after my actual abilities. If it took me longer to learn choreography, if I messed up a step during a routine, if I stumbled during warm-up, anything. He zeroed in on me and gave me hell, like I was the *only* one who ever messed up."

"Where was your teacher during all this? What did your mom do?" I growl, unable to contain it any longer, balling my fists as I picture throttling the little shit who tortured Vi into thinking she was anything less than perfect.

"Oh, he got into trouble every time he did it. Time out, scolding, that sort of thing. And to me, my teacher would just say that boys are mean to girls when they like them. But that never made me feel any better. And my mom raised hell at my school when I'd come home crying, but then I just got picked on for being a baby who ran home and tattled to my mommy, so I stopped telling her," she says, making my gut twist when I realize she started taking the blows all on her own, hiding it from her mom.

I've taken as much as I can stand, giving her space to open up and tell me about the part of herself she keeps hidden. I reach over, grab the chain of her swing, and pull her to me, sitting her—seat and all— in my lap as I wrap my arms around her middle. "I can promise you one thing, baby girl. No one will ever say another unkind thing to you without having to deal with me. If anyone ever says a hateful word to you again, you tell me. And you will never have to worry about them giving you shit for it afterward either, because it'll be hard for them to tease you with their tongue ripped out of their head." She makes a sound, half giggle and half surprised squeak, as if she thinks what I said is funny, but can't figure out if I'm exaggerating. I'm not. "Promise you'll tell me, Vi," I demand.

She blinks up at me, clearing her vision. "I promise, Corbin," she whispers, and I lean down, pressing my lips gently to hers, not attempting to take the kiss further. Now is not the time to push her. I'll give her time to come to me when she's ready to take our physical relationship to the next level. From the sound of it, she's had enough assholes pushing her around to last her a lifetime. The last thing she needs is me coercing her into doing something she's not ready for.

"Knowing you've got me by your side, no matter what, you think you might be able to let go of some of your fears?" I breathe against her lips, pressing my forehead to hers.

After a brief pause, in which I can tell she truly thinks about her answer, she whispers, "Yeah. I think I can."

Warmth spreads throughout my chest. Feeling the weight of the moment, I try to lighten the mood, the seriousness of the past few minutes too heavy to end our first date on. "I'm glad. Your first driving lesson is tomorrow then... my beautiful girlfriend." I grin, seeing her face scrunch up as I pull back to look at her.

"Ugh. Fine. You can ask Mom if we can use her car when you take me home, *boyfriend*," she concedes.

"Good girl," I tell her, giving her a light swat on the ass as I slide her off my lap and let her swing away. I stand and hold out my hand to her, and when she takes it, I pull her out of the seat. "Let's get you home."

"But it's still early," she says quietly, and I love the disappointment I hear there, knowing she doesn't want this night to end either.

"I know. But think of the brownie points I'll earn with your dad for bringing you home way before curfew. Plus, I'm going to come over bright and early tomorrow. After you get comfortable, you can drive us to Rock On, and we can make up for some of the hours you missed climbing today while you were being threatened with spankings."

BEFORE THE lie

Seven

Vi

MY HEART POUNDS INSIDE my chest, and I place my trembling hand on the shifter, pressing the brake with my foot so I can move it into drive.

"Nice and easy, baby girl. We're just gonna do a couple of laps around the school," Corbin tells me, and I lift my foot off the brake and move it over to the gas. The car begins to roll forward without me pressing the pedal, and I wonder for a minute if it would be acceptable just to let the car drift around the building going three miles per hour. "Give her a little gas," he orders, cutting off that hopeful train of thought.

I can't believe Mom agreed to let us use her car, no questions asked. After a sweet kiss on my doorstep, I'd opened my front door last night just as Mom was coming out of the kitchen, and seeing Corbin there on the porch, she'd come over to tell him goodnight. He asked her simply, "Would it be all right if we used your car so I can take Vi to practice driving tomorrow? I'd happily let her use mine, but I have a manual, and she told me no."

"No problem, sweetheart," she told him, and after thanking her, he turned to me with a smirk and a wink before telling me goodnight, kissing me on the cheek, and heading out to his car. If he weren't so freakin' sexy, my palm would've itched to smack him.

So here we are now, in the parking lot of the high school near my neighborhood—what would be my home school if I didn't go to a private one. It's Sunday, so it's completely deserted.

I press the gas gently and get the car going a little faster. It's been two and a half years since I took Driver's Ed, and the same length of time since I sat in a driver's seat. I had no desire to be in control of a moving vehicle, the responsibility feeling way too overwhelming. But Corbin was right. I can't depend on other people to get me where I need to go for the rest of my life. And with him by my side, I feel a little bit of his strength and a whole lot of his protectiveness seeping into me as I begin my second lap around the school.

"Okay, great. Now, you ready to take it on the road? We can just drive around your neighborhood if you want. Nothing crazy yet," he suggests, and I take a deep breath and nod.

I stop fully and look both ways at the parking lot's exit, and seeing no one coming, I pull out onto the empty road, traveling only a few yards before putting my left turn signal on and turning into my neighborhood. I get up to the speed limit, 25 miles per hour, and follow each of his instructions, when he tells me to take a left at the next stop sign, or a right in the fork. I do a

U-turn in a cul-de-sac, and we practice parking, backing up, and three-point turns.

After another fifteen minutes of this, with my confidence building higher and higher with his words of encouragement and praise, he tells me, "It's almost time for the gym to open. Your mom has my car if she needs to go anywhere today, and she said it was okay with her if you felt comfortable enough to drive hers to Rock On. She'll meet us there later to switch cars."

"Couldn't you just take me home?" I ask, trying to stall before making my final decision on whether or not I have the balls to drive across town for the first time.

"Not tonight, baby girl. The gym is much closer to the base than your house, and I've got to be up before the sun tomorrow for PT. Not unless you want to quit climbing early this evening," he offers, but I shake my head.

"No. That's okay. I want to climb as much as I can tonight, since I didn't go at all yesterday," I reply, my grip tightening on the steering wheel.

"I figured as much. Okay. You've got this, Vi. Just go the speed limit, if not slower if you're scared. But I've got you. Not going to let anything happen to us. We'll take the back roads your mom told me about, so you won't even have to get out on the busy main streets if you don't want to," he assures, and I nod.

After twenty minutes, five minutes longer than it normally takes to get to the gym from my house, I pull into the parking lot of Rock On, my blood pumping with my racing pulse as if I just won a national climbing competition. I ease into a parking spot, put the car in park, and turn to Corbin, my whole body trembling with unspent adrenaline.

My eyes lift to meet his proud ones sparkling down at me,

and the look is my undoing, as I tell him, "I need something, Corbin."

"What do you need, baby girl?" he asks, his eyebrows lowering in confusion.

"I... I don't like this jittery feeling. I need it out of me," I tell him, my voice a little shaky as I try to figure out a way to convey what my body is demanding.

"Do you feel like you're going to have a panic attack? What is it, Vi? You need some air? Let's get you out of the ca—"

"No!" I shout, wincing at my volume in the enclosed space, repeating "No," in a much quieter voice. "I... I'm already past that wanting to run feeling, and at the part where I'm ready to be a little reckless and just say eff it and try something new for the first time. The fight feeling instead of the flight, yeah?" I implore him with my eyes, begging him to get what I'm saying. "Th-that stuff you were saying last night...."

Suddenly, understanding blankets his face, and his eyes go soft. "I got you, baby," he murmurs, unhooking his seatbelt before reaching across the console to do the same to mine.

My eyes never leave his as I feel the tight belt disappear from across my body, until I feel his hot, strong hand wrap around the back of my neck and he pulls me to him. And the next thing I feel is his breath against my lips, as he whispers, "I fell asleep when I got home from our date, thinking about this very moment, Vi. Then, my night was filled with dreams of kissing you, of getting to taste my girl for the first time. Of being the very first man to ever *get* to taste you. I want your first *real* kiss to be one you remember until your dying day."

My world tilts on its axis, and I feel dizzy listening to his intense words, my adrenaline pumping and my pulse pounding, so with my eyes still closed, I reach up to grip his muscled forearm to ground myself. "Corbin, please. Dyno," I beg, hoping he gets me.

Finally, with a growl that reverberates from his chest and shoots straight to my core, he takes my lips possessively with his. After a moment, I gasp as he bites down on my bottom lip, his tongue dipping in, and I taste Corbin for the very first time, savoring it as he seemed to do in his dream.

With a whimper, I tentatively flick the underside of his tongue with mine, and he lets loose another growl, tilting our heads to deepen the kiss. I'm enveloped in an all-consuming bubble of sensuality, memorizing everything from the sound of his quiet groan, to the heat of his mouth against mine, to the taste of... him. Just Corbin.

I feel him subtly guiding my movements, as if leading me in an erotic dance of tongues and panted breath. And now that I've finally taken this leap of faith, I never want this feeling of flight to stop. I soar higher and higher with every stroke, every flex of his strong fingers around my nape, every moan that escapes, until I feel like I've flown so high I've reached the sun. My body is ablaze as I give myself over to Corbin, showing him I'm putting all my trust in him and that I want him to teach me everything he's willing to.

We devour each other for what feels like forever yet no time at all, and when we finally pull back from each other, we're both out of breath and flushed. As I meet his eyes, they swarm with all the emotions I feel inside myself, and it's a comfort that our kiss affected him just as much as it did me.

He pulls me back toward him, but only to rest his forehead against mine, as he whispers, "Never letting you go now, baby girl. That kiss just sealed our fate. You're mine."

The little hairs on my arms stand up as my skin prickles before a feeling of warmth washes over me. All I can do is nod, as I pray that he always feels this way about me, because it's exactly what I feel for him.

Eight

Corbin

THE NEXT MONTH AND A half passes in a blur. Every moment I'm not at work or sleeping is spent with Vi. From the second I get off work in the evenings until the rock gym closes at night, we spend it climbing, Vi teaching me techniques that have improved my skills tenfold, while I return the favor with strength training. It's amazing what it's done for her self-confidence, both seeing me as her student get better and better at my climbing, and also as her teacher, who has made her work hard and gotten her to the point where she can now do ten pull-ups, when before she could only do one.

I've been lucky enough to have weekends off for a while now, and they've been spent together, going to countless movies, trying out every restaurant in town, and venturing a little ways to go to the history museum an hour away. It's been blissful, nothing standing in our way as we learn everything about each other. She comes to life under my touch. She's still too shy to initiate anything intimate between us, but I have no problem taking control and giving her what I know she wants but is too submissive to ask for. Nothing past the best kisses I've ever had in my entire life, but she's worth the wait.

Our... courtship, I guess you would call it, has been so different from any relationship I had in the past. Almost as if we're living in a different era. We've taken our time reaching each milestone, making each one special, instead of rushing to get to the immediate gratification of going all the way. The first hug, the first date, the first peck, the first passion-filled kiss with tongue... every marker has been distinct, had its own story, its own memory to look back on and cherish separately from all the rest. For once in my life, I feel like I'm doing something right, outside my job.

Our two personalities seem to have been made for each other. I can read her like a book, knowing what she needs from me when she can't seem to figure out what it is she actually wants. It keeps the dominant inside me satisfied having so much power over her needs, being able to please her without her having to say a word. He puffs up his chest and struts, feeling like her savior, her knight in shining armor, after a lifetime of feeling like a worthless asshole who couldn't do anything right. It soothes my soul, much like her sweetness. The way she looks at me, like I hung the moon and every single one of those stars we saw in the perfectly clear sky that night in the park, it makes me want to be the man she sees me as.

I've heard lots of those inspirational quotes on relationships, but never paid much attention to them until now. "Be the man your dog thinks you are." "Be with the person who gives you the same feeling you get when you see your food coming at a restaurant." Or the one that really hits home when it comes to Vi and me, "A perfect relationship is just two imperfect people who refuse to give up on each other." God knows we both have our flaws, but we seem to fit each other like jigsaw puzzle pieces, filling in the gaps of each other. Her softness cushions my roughness. My overabundance of fearlessness spills into her over-cautiousness, making her braver. At the same time, it pulls me back, making me take a second to think about the consequences of actions I wouldn't have taken the time to worry about before. Two imperfect people, with too little of some characteristics and too much of others, but then we come together and we are a perfect balance.

As I said, bliss. But I got some news today that didn't make me very happy, yet I suppose it'll be our first lesson in the military life causing disappointment in our relationship. I just hope Vi doesn't take it too rough.

When she finishes her route inside the cave we've been climbing in for the last hour, I take hold of her hand and pull her down next to me in the regrind I've been sitting in while I watched her boulder. "Gotta talk to you, baby girl," I murmur, wrapping my arm around her hips to pull her side flush with mine.

"What is it?" Her eyes immediately fill with worry, and I hate that I am the one who put it there.

I reach up and tuck the fallen strands of her hair behind her ear. "I just found out my unit will be going into the field for training for three weeks. The bad news is while I'm out there,

there is no communication. No phones, no email, nothing," I tell her, and she visibly wilts at this information. "Also, worse news, it takes place during your graduation as well. I'm so fucking sorry I have to miss that, Vi. I know you wanted me to be there, but there's nothing I can do."

She looks down in her lap and nods. After a moment, she asks quietly, "That was the bad news, so what's the good news?"

"Well, the good news is that at some point during the three weeks, I'll get a few days completely off in the middle of the week. I'll have to do twenty-four hours of straight guard duty at the barracks one day, but then I'll get time off to do whatever the hell we want, and I'll take you wherever your heart desires to make up for missing your walk across the stage." I squeeze her hip, and her eyes lift to mine.

"Can we go to Six Flags?" She tilts her head, her face full of hope that I'll say yes, and I grin.

"Anywhere in the world, and you want to go to an amusement park?" I chuckle.

"I told you I love roller coasters," she says with a shrug.

"Then that's what we'll do." I lean over and kiss her, making her smile and some of the disappointment leaves her face as she glances away.

"That's actually way less terrible than what I thought you were going to say," she confesses, and my brows lower.

"What did you think I wanted to talk about?" I question.

She sighs. "I always have this tiny voice in the back of my head that says any day now you're going to realize I'm nothing special and—"

"Not another word, Vi," I growl, taking her jaw in my hand and forcing her eyes to meet mine once more. "Nothing pisses me off faster than when I hear you putting yourself down." Her face falls, but I don't back down. She needs to hear this. "*You* are amazing. *You* are the one who is too good for *me*. You make me want to be a better man, one who deserves you. So never let me hear you say you're nothing special, because there's no one else who could've gotten me to learn patience. Or self-control. Or how to care about anyone other than myself." My grip tightens, wanting to make sure she pays close attention to what I'm about to say, because it's the most important thing that will ever come out of my mouth. "Just stay loyal to me, my beautiful Vi, and you will never have to worry about that stupid-ass voice in the back of your head being right. Got it?"

She bites her bottom lip and her eyes go soft, and I can't tell if she actually realizes when she says it, but she whispers, "Yes, sir," and my cock swells inside my basketball shorts. I drag her into my lap, sitting her soft ass directly onto my erection to soothe some of the throbbing as it's sandwiched between my body and hers.

I tug her face down to mine with a hand tangled at the back of her hair, and kiss the breath out of her. And I don't let up until we're interrupted by Sierra calling, "Get a room, you two!" from the mouth of the cave.

I allow Vi to slide off my lap, and I adjust myself, bringing her eyes to my painfully hard cock. She unconsciously licks her lips, red and swollen from my assault, and I growl deep from within my chest. "You keep looking at it like that, baby girl, and you're going to make me eat my words about having patience and self-control." I watch her eyes widen when she sees me grasp my shaft, giving it a brief squeeze to ease some of the ache. She lets out a soft gasp, my size and shape no longer left to the imagination, clearly visible through the soft fabric of my shorts, and I groan, the sound pained, even to my own ears.

Her eyes meet mine, worry filling them yet again. "Does it hurt, Corbin?" she whispers, and the concern in her voice puts another stitch in my previously ripped soul. God, with as much *bad* as I have done in my life, how the hell did I manage to find and fall for someone so undeniably *good*?

"It could feel better, baby girl. But I'll survive." I give her a soft smile before leaning over to steal a gentle kiss from her pouted lips, and then get to my feet, adjusting my hard-on to sit behind the waistband of my shorts. Her eyes flare then dart away when she catches a glimpse of the swollen head before I cover it with my black T-shirt, and I can't help but smirk, knowing mine is the first cock she ever had a peek at in the flesh.

Face red and a voice breathy, she tells me it's my turn to try out the ceiling route. Without a word, deciding not to tease her, I get into starting position.

Vi

IT'S BEEN TWO WEEKS since Corbin went into the field. I've tried to keep myself busy, sticking with the routine I had the four years before he came into my life. But now that he's in it, I can't help the emptiness I feel without him there.

I used to be completely content, spending hours climbing by myself, with no one there to hang out with except my mom. But now... now I find myself constantly listening out for the jingle of the bell above the door, when before I barely paid attention to it. Now, I brace myself for an excited whoop and to be spun in the air by massive and protective arms whenever I finish a super hard route, when before, just my satisfaction of knowing I did it was enough.

It's a double-edged sword. But as lonely as I feel right now without him with me, I wouldn't want to go back to the way it was before. I might have been content in my self-imposed solitude, but I didn't know happiness until I met Corbin.

I had no clue when his break would be during the three-week training, in which he explained was out in the wilderness of Ft. Vanter. He just said he'd call as soon as he got his hands on a phone to let me know he was in from the field to pull his 24-hour guard duty, and then after that, I'd have him all to myself for a couple of days before he went back out to finish training.

A part of me had expected his call to come a lot sooner than this. And that evil little voice in the back of my head kept trying to whisper that maybe he just didn't want to see me, so he hadn't called like he promised. But I always push it back, choosing to trust Corbin, to believe what he said when he told me that as long as I stay loyal to him, then he'd never have a reason to leave. I scoff every time I think about it. I would never in a million years cheat on anyone, and the thought of ever doing that to Corbin, the only man who has ever made me *feel* anything, is completely ridiculous. So I guess he's stuck with me.

Graduation was last night. I actually hadn't been too upset that Corbin missed it, because I didn't want him to be there to see I had no friends to hug after we threw our caps in the air, or feel sorry for me when no one clapped. My brother had driven up from Charleston for the day to see me walk. I had dreaded crossing the stage, expecting to hear nothing but crickets chirping after the principal called my name, but with Mom, Dad, and Henry in the crowd, they made as much ruckus as even the most popular graduates' families, making me laugh as I got back to my seat.

Tonight, I lay restless in my bed, unable to fall asleep, so I chose an old favorite off my small bookshelf and began to read about sexy shifters and their loveable heroines.

My eyelids are finally beginning to get heavy, and I'm just about to bookmark my page as I read the last one in the chapter, when my cell suddenly rings, making me jump and drop the paperback right on my face.

"Shit!" I hiss, and then realize I hit the green answer button with my arm in my fight with the book. "He-hello?" I sit up in bed, rubbing the bridge of my nose.

"Baby girl, you okay?" Corbin's voice comes through my phone, and immediately the bit of pain I felt disappears as a feeling of pure joy washes through me.

"Corbin!" I squeal, hopping up on my bed.

"Vi, you all right?" he asks, and I hear a door slam closed in the background.

"Yeah! Your call just startled me. I was reading and dropped my book on my face." I laugh. "Did you just get in? I've missed you so much!" My heart pounds with my excitement, and any tiredness I felt before has completely vanished.

"God, I've missed you too, baby. I just got to the barracks. I have half a mind to come see y—"

"Do it!" I cut in, the words flying out of my mouth without my permission, and I bite my lip, snorting. "Sorry. I was literally drifting off to sleep, but then the phone scared me and now I'm all jittery."

"You were just now falling asleep? It's like one in the morning," he points out, and I hear him climbing stairs.

I plop down on the bed, pulling my covers over my naked legs. "I haven't been able to fall asleep very well since you've been out there," I admit quietly.

"Aw, Vi...." There's a pause, and then I make out the sound of a door opening and closing before I hear his voice much more clearly, as he stops moving. "If you truly want me to, I will drive over there to see you. God knows I'd give anything just to hold you for even a moment. My 24-hour shift starts in two hours. And then after I get some sleep when it's over, you and I are going to Six Flags. Just say the word, baby girl, and I'm there in thirty."

As much as I want to be selfish and tell him to come see me, even for a brief moment, just knowing he kept his word and called me the second he got in is enough to soothe me until I see him after his guard duty. "No, Corbin. That's okay. Get you a nap in before your shift starts. I'm so glad you're back. I've missed you *terribly*," I sob the last word, the roller coaster of emotions in the past few minutes crashing down on me, making me feel weepy. I also just got off my period, so that could be a factor in why I suddenly feel like crying I'm so happy he's home.

"You sure you're okay, Vi?" he questions, his voice soft and concerned.

"I'm sure. I promise. I'm just being a girl." I laugh, waving away his worry, even though he can't see the gesture. "It really is so wonderful to hear your voice." My own comes out dreamy as I lie back down, turning over on my side.

"Yours too, baby. I can't wait to see you. Just one more day and a handful of hours, all right? And I'll be the only one here, guarding my empty building tomorrow, so I'll be able to text you all day. Then I'm all yours for two days."

I hear shuffling, as if he's removing his clothes then getting into bed, and heat fills my chest then spreads lower, thinking about the part of his body I'd caught a glimpse of in the climbing cave. "O-okay," I reply, my voice coming out husky.

"Vi?"

"Yeah?" I breathe, my eyes closing, imaging what Corbin would look like right now, undressed and lying in his bed as he talks to me.

"What are you thinking about that's got your voice sounding like that?" he inquires, his own voice going low and deep.

"I... I... I'm just wondering what you look like right now, is all," I confess, my face heating to match the fire spreading toward the place between my legs. I cross my thighs, trying to tamp out the inferno starting to blaze there.

I hear him exhale a moment, before he replies in his sexy, gruff voice, "I just took off my boots and my BDUs. I've been in the field for two weeks without an actual shower, but me and the boys jumped into the lake today, so I'm a lot cleaner than I was." He groans, and I hear movement, as if he's getting comfortable in his bed. "My whole body is sore from all the training we've done, and I've got a few scrapes and bruises from being out in the woods, but otherwise, I look just the same as I did the last time you saw me. Just... naked."

As he says the last word, my core clenches, imagining him lying there in his bed, a blanket with an outdoor scene beneath him, the glorious parts of his body I've already seen—those beautifully muscled arms, the top of his tattooed chest, his strong calves, the bulging head of his erection—perfectly clear in my mind's eye, while my imagination fills in the rest I haven't. "Oh...." I breathe.

"What about you? What are you wearing?"

God, the tone of his voice is like an injection of liquid fire into my veins as it makes a roadmap beneath every inch of my skin.

I glance down, feeling suddenly naked, even though I'm in what I normally wear to bed. I can't help but giggle. "My favorite lavender long night shirt and undies. Sorry, nothing special. Only thing sexy about it is the Victoria's Secret label." I roll my eyes. *Could you be any more of a turn-off, Vi?*

He groans, a delicious sound from deep within his chest, and my cheeks flush. "No, baby girl. Sexy as fuck. Sweet and innocent, like you," he whispers, and his breath comes out in a shudder.

Is he...?

"Corbin?"

"Yeah, baby?" His voice sounds distant.

"You... you falling asleep?" I ask, because there's no way I could bring myself to ask if he's doing what I *really* think he's doing.

"Far from it," he exhales.

I hold my breath, listening intently, trying to let the sounds on the other end of the line paint a picture inside my head. I imagine his perfect face, eyes closed, his lips parted, and then his chest rising and falling with every pant I hear. "Do you want me to let you go?" I offer quietly, feeling like a voyeur, as if I'm intruding on a very personal act. The feeling isn't quite uncomfortable, but almost. Like I'm peeking in on something I know I shouldn't, but I just can't look away.

"No," he growls, and it sounds more like a command to stay

on the phone rather than an answer to my question.

"Well... what do you want to talk ab—"

"Are you wet for me, Vi?" he groans, and my heart thuds in my chest.

"Wh-what?" I squirm beneath my covers, feeling exposed and vulnerable.

"I'm so hard right now, baby girl, thinking about finally seeing you, kissing you, wrapping you up in my arms. God, I can almost imagine the smell of you. Tell me, Vi, are you as wet as I am hard?" The question comes out as a demand, and my natural reaction is to give him what he wants. It's always my response to him, wanting to give him exactly what he asks of me, no questions asked.

"I... I don't know," I reply honestly. My thighs squeeze together, trying to relieve some of the growing ache there, the feeling still new, having only experienced it since I met Corbin, yet I have no clue what to do about it.

"Touch yourself, baby. Tell me exactly what you feel," he commands, and my hand grips the soft fabric of my T-shirt's hem.

"Corbin, I... I don't know how to do that," I confess softly, feeling awkward but completely turned on.

"Vi," he groans. "Are you telling me you've never gotten yourself off before?"

"Of course I haven't," I whine. "I only started feeling any type of... anything down there when I met you. So why would I have ever... touched it?"

"Oh, fuck," he growls, and I bite my lip, thinking I'm somehow in trouble, which I know is ridiculous. After a few moments of listening to his ragged breath, I hear movement before he settles back down. "Like a fucking schoolboy. Swear to Christ."

"What's wrong?" I ask, confused.

"Your untouched little pussy, baby girl," he tells me, and I suck in a sharp breath, my entire body flushing at the vulgar word. "You made me come just thinking about the fact that it's never been touched, not even by you. I had wanted to hear you make yourself come, but knowing you've never done that is somehow even hotter."

I don't know what to say. I want him to stop talking, to stop making me feel this way, but at the same time I don't. I feel special instead of like an inexperienced freak. Desired. *Alive.*

"I can't wait to make you mine, baby girl. I'll wait forever for you, but God... I can't wait to feel you. To make you feel good. To bring you pleasure you've never experienced before," he says quietly. Thankfully, he continues, saving me from having to stutter out a response. "But I'm going to pass out until my shift now. I'll text you soon."

"Okay, Corbin," I whisper. "Goodnight."

"Night." And the line goes silent.

I SPEND THE ENTIRE next day at Rock On, trying to pass the time by climbing while texting with Corbin between routes. We spend his lunch hour talking on the phone, excited about tomorrow. We plan on him picking me up bright and early to make the four-hour drive there. I tell him he should sleep in after his long shift, but he swears that five hours will be plenty, so to be ready around eight.

I'm eating the Whopper Mom brought me for lunch, when Sierra plops down on the picnic bench opposite me, stealing a French fry. "So... when do you want to start working?" she asks, popping the fry in her mouth.

"Maybe after school lets out. The week Climbing Camp starts?" I suggest. "I want a week or two just to feel what it's like being out of high school."

"Uh huh... more like you want a week or two to be at your boyfriend's beck and call," she teases, and I toss a fry at her face. She catches it and eats that one too. "I'm just playing. Speaking out of pure jealousy. Your man is freaking eye candy. You two must go at it like bunnies constantly."

My face heats and I look over at my mom, who's absorbed in her book on the couch about twenty feet away. Balling up the wrapper that had been around my burger, I avoid responding.

"Oh... em gee. Vi," she hisses.

"What?" I hiss back.

"You're as easy to read as a large-print book. Have y'all not done it yet?"

"Uh..."

"Vivian. Marie. Brown. How in the hell have you been able to keep your hands off of *that?*" she whisper-yells, leaning over the table. "You've been inseparable for almost three months!"

"Well, seeing how I've kept my hands off everyone, including myself, it hasn't been that hard," I tell her quietly, and watch her face turn completely shocked. "Yeah, apparently that's super crazy to people. Corbin had an equivalent response."

"You told your boyfriend that you've never masturbated before? God, to be a fly on the wall to see his reaction." She shakes her head.

"How the hell did we get on this subject? Why are we talking about my sex life? This is so not appropriate coworker conversation," I say haughtily, cleaning up the bits of lettuce that had fallen off my lunch.

"Oh, shut up. We're much more than coworkers, and you know it," she tells me, throwing a French fry at me this time.

I look up into her pretty face, tilting my head. I hadn't actually thought about it before, since I've never seen Sierra outside of Rock On before, but now that she's pointed it out, I guess she is my one and only real friend. Conversation has always come easy with her. She's always been incredibly nice to me, not a mean bone in her tall and curvy body. We've spent what adds up to be countless hours together over the years, just chatting and hanging out in the gym during my rest breaks. I don't know why I never considered it before. Maybe because she's a few years older than me, or the fact she's married with a baby, at a much different stage in her life than I was, so I just never thought of her as anything more than an acquaintance.

"Geez, Vi. I knew you were super devoted to your sport, but wow. How have you made it this long without ever double-clicking the mouse?"

"Huh?" My eyebrows scrunch.

"You know... tiptoeing through the two lips. Buffin' the muffin. A little ménage à moi." At my confused face, she finally hisses, "How the hell have you never fingerbanged yourself, woman? You're eighteen!"

I shrug, feeling surprisingly comfortable confiding in her, now that I've come to the realization I actually have a girlfriend to talk about this stuff with. "I never had a need for it. I never wanted anyone before I met Corbin. I was always so focused on climbing I never really paid attention to anything that would've made me... get an urge," I whisper the last bit, even though there are no climbers near our table.

"Hmm." She leans back, reaching out and pulling the bag of fries with her, and starts to munch on them while she ponders something. "But you said you told Corbin about it. I assume you're still a virgin then. Because now that I think about it, God knows you don't spend enough time away from this place to even sneak in a quickie."

"Yes, I'm still a virgin. But...."

"But what?" she prompts.

I tilt toward her, my eyes squinting in concentration as I try to put into words what I haven't spoken aloud. "I... I think I'm ready *not* to be," I murmur, and her face splits into a beautiful smile.

"Well, you couldn't have picked a better guy to lose it to. The way he looks at you... gosh." She giggles, shaking her head.

"What do you mean?"

"Aww. Sweet Vi. You really have no idea, do you?" At my disgruntled face, she chuckles and continues. "When that man looks at you... it's like that emoji, the smiley face with hearts for eyes. Just like that. He's totally head over heels for you. No question."

I bite my lip for a moment. "I mean... I hoped what I saw wasn't just my imagination. But... really? That's what you see too?"

"Oh. Girl. Absolutely. And the way he wards off other guys with just that super sexy scary look. He's totally marked you as his territory," she says, waving her hand in the air nonchalantly.

"What are you talking about?" I ask, genuinely having no clue what she's referring to.

"Dude. For real? I'm going to start calling you Cher, because you are totes clueless. When you're up on the wall, and people come over to watch you, you do realize that you've got most of those guys bonered-up, right?" I cock an eyebrow, and she rolls her eyes. "There is not a guy who comes in here who doesn't want to bang you against one of these rock-covered walls. They get one look at your tiny self going all Spidergirl, and their tongues practically roll right out of their heads. But ever since you and Corbin got together, one glance from him, and they all back away, exposing their vulnerable necks to him or some shit. He's definitely an alpha. *Ah-ooooo*," she howls, and I can't help but laugh.

"But like I said, if you feel you're ready, there's no way it would be anything but perfect. He takes such care with you *now*. I can't even imagine how good he'd be to you intimately. Plus, I saw you two making out in the cave. Y'all's nookie is going to be hot as fuck, giiiirl. Yaaas, honey!" she whisper-sings to me as she stands, throwing the empty fry bag into the brown paper bag all my food came in. She swishes her hips as she makes her way around to my side of the table, then leans down to my ear. "If you need to talk about anything, I'm always here, girlfriend. Muah!" She plants a hard kiss to the side of my head, and then prances to the front of the gym.

I smile, warm all over from the sweet feeling of having a real friend.

BEFORE THE *lie*
BEFORE THE *lie*
BEFORE THE *lie*
RE THE *lie*
lie

Nine

Vi

THIS MORNING'S REUNION with Corbin was almost painful. As he stepped out of his Camaro in my driveway, I slammed into him so hard that even he stumbled back a step as I wrapped my entire body, arms and legs, around him like a spider monkey.

"There's my girl," he whispered in my ear, his arms wrapping around me to squeeze me to him. "God, I've missed you, baby."

I pulled back just enough to look into his eyes, so happy to see him in the flesh, and he reached up with one hand to pull my face down to his, kissing me right there in the driveway.

We spent the day riding rollercoasters and eating giant turkey legs, but most enjoyable of all, just holding hands as we walked through the amusement park and flirting playfully while we stood in line for rides. Being the middle of the week, we basically had the place to ourselves except for a couple school field trips taking place there, so we were able to ride everything we wanted multiple times, and left before the sun went down.

Halfway home, Corbin clears his throat and adjusts in his leather seat as he drives. "So... we got done a lot earlier than expected. Do you want to do something when we get back?" he asks.

"Sure, like what?" I turn sideways in my seat, my left leg coming up beneath my right, and admire his profile. The masculine ridge of his brow countering the almost feminine pout of his full lips, his straight nose, and his killer jawline, which is now dark with a five o'clock shadow. I can barely look at him he's so handsome when he's clean shaven, but when he's got that bit of facial hair at the end of the day, and even more on the weekends when he doesn't have to work, jeez, he's irresistible—if I would ever gain the courage to tell him I'm ready....

"Well, there aren't any movies out I want to see at the theater. Do you want to rent one and take it to my room?" he suggests, and my head tilts.

"Like... at the barracks?" I question. When he gives me an, "Mmm-hmm," I add, "I thought chicks weren't allowed in the barracks."

"No, chicks in *high school* aren't allowed in the barracks. But as of this past weekend, you are officially a high school graduate now, baby girl." He smiles lightly and glances in the rearview mirror before eyeing me for a moment. "It doesn't matter to me what we do. I'm just not ready for this day to end. If you don't want to—"

"No!" I cut him off. "I do. You just caught me a little off guard is all. I'd love to go see where you live."

He chuckles. "It's nothing to see. But it is somewhere quiet and private we can go to just be by ourselves. I like having you all to myself."

My heart drops into my stomach and is swarmed by butterflies at the thought of being alone with Corbin... just the two of us... in his room... on his bed.... I glance outside, seeing on a sign we're sixty-three miles from Ft. Vanter. A little over an hour before we get home—no, not home. *Corbin's* room. Why couldn't he have asked me this when we were closer? When I had less time to sit and dwell on what could happen while we're alone... just the two of us... in his room... on his be—

"Vi?" His deep voice reverberates through the interior of his Camaro. "No pressure, baby," he tells me, staring into my eyes before facing forward once again.

The tension in me releases somewhat. God, could he be any more perfect? It's like he's tuned in to me, sensing everything inside me, even when I know I do a damn good job of hiding it. But at the same time, he still hasn't read my mind, broadcasting telepathically that I want him. Or maybe he's receiving my mixed signals. My emotions are everywhere. I want desperately for him to take me, to make love to me, to make me his in every way. But the thought of it actually happening scares the shit out of me.

I wish he would take control, ignore my nerves he's picking up on, and just rip off the Band-Aid, so to speak. I'm entirely too intimidated and inexperienced to voice or even passive-aggressively show that I'm ready to have sex for the first time, to give him my virginity. All he'd have to do is make the first move, give me any opening, and I would make it clear to him that I'm all for it. Just kiss me deeply, and I would pour myself into the kiss and not let go until he understood. It's just the lead-up that's terrifying.

"What movie do you want to watch?" he asks me, obviously trying to bring me out of my stupor, and I shake myself, realizing I had been staring straight through him.

"A comedy. Definitely a comedy," I reply.

"What, you don't want to watch a scary movie, where you'll have to cling to me to keep you safe from the boogie man?" he teases, tickling up my leg, making me squeal.

"I don't do scary movies. My brother traumatized me when I was little." I pout. "He was supposed to take me to see a Disney movie, but we went into *Gothica* instead. At first, I thought it was cool I was going to see a grown-up movie with my big brother, but an hour in, he thought it would be funny to grab me right at the crescendo of a scary part, and it frightened me so bad I screamed and peed, right there in the chair. I avoid horror movies at all costs now."

The confession is worth every ounce of embarrassment, as Corbin throws back his head and lets out one of his rare belly laughs. I feel it to the very depths of my soul. It doesn't happen often, so when I can make him laugh like that, when he lets his guard down and shows every bit of his amusement, I feel so accomplished and happy that I can make him feel that way for a few moments. It's not often my serious soldier gets to be carefree, so when I get to witness these fleeting seconds, I take a mental picture of the look on his face, and try to record the sound of his laugh to play back later, because God only knows when he could be sent somewhere.

These weeks he's spent training in the field have been hard enough. I don't know what I'll do with myself if and when he ever gets deployed. So I try to capture the tiny dimple that forms on one side of his lips when he smiles this big. The gasp of breath he takes between bouts of laughter. The tiny line that forms between his eyebrows, and the even smaller ones at the corners of his sparkling brown eyes.

When he finally catches his breath, he looks over at me, and heat joins the sparkles in his gaze. "If you keep looking at me like that, baby girl, I'm going to have to pull this car over and have my way with you," he growls, his sight zeroing in on my mouth, where I was unconsciously biting my bottom lip as I watched him.

"Please do," I breathe, and then my eyes widen when I realize I said it out loud.

He lifts his eyes to mine and his brow furrows. Time seems to stand still as he stares at me with that intense stare. I feel as if he is looking into my very soul, reading into my two slipped words. *Yes*, I implore, *I mean it.*

"Are you ready, baby girl?" he asks, his eyes never wavering from mine.

The tension grows even more potent, and it forces me to glance toward the road. I'm fascinated the car stays perfectly centered between the lines of the open road, even as I feel his intense look boring into the side of my face. I take a deep breath in through my nose, let it out slowly through my mouth, inhale once more before I turn back to him, wet my lips with the tip of my tongue... and dyno.

"I am."

Corbin

I WATCHED CAREFULLY as Vi gained her courage, much like she does before a tricky move on the rocks, and when she turned to me and said those two words, *I am*, her voice was steady, strong, and determined.

I'd used self-control I didn't know I possessed, when it came to her. Although I usually never had to try to pursue a woman for very long in order to take her to bed—if at all, seeing how I got hit on the majority of the time, not the other way around—I hadn't tried to get her to move any faster than her own pace. I waited for clues, letting me know she wanted me to kiss her, when with anyone else I would've done it whenever *I* wanted.

The only things she seems courageous enough to do herself are placing her tiny hand in mine to hold while we walk, or sit in movie theaters, playful swats while we joke around, and the occasional hug that she initiates. But every kiss to date has been me giving it to her, not her taking. Part of me wonders if she is that naturally submissive, while the rest of me believes it's just fear from being so inexperienced. Yet the way she just answered my question left no room for doubt that she wants me, and I'm not about to give her a chance to change her mind.

Pressing down on the gas, my speed goes from a steady cruise of fifty-five miles per hour up to ninety, and I hear her sweet giggle from beside me. She loves going fast in my Camaro. And I know she loves watching me shift gears by the way she always bites her lip while her eyes follow my right hand on the stick. I don't often get to race around with her in our small town, but out here, on the deserted back road we took to get to and from the amusement park four hours away, I open it up and give her a thrill.

I hear her gasp, but I don't take my eyes off the road. "Corbin! You're going a hundred!" she squeaks.

"Hundred and eight, actually," I correct, and feel her swat my arm.

"Slow down! You're going to get a ticket."

"Radar detector says otherwise, baby. Hasn't beeped in the last three hours. Now, grab my stick."

"*Excuse* me?" she scoffs, and I laugh.

"The stick shift, perv."

"Why?" she asks suspiciously.

I grab her hand and put it on the black knob of the gear shifter, then cover it with my palm. "Ready?"

"For what? What are you doing?" she asks, her voice panicked.

"Down to fourth," I say, and we downshift into the lower gear, slowing down a little. "Third." Our hands move again, and the car slows even further. "Second." The trees outside stop whizzing past as our speed lowers until I finish with, "First," before bringing the Camaro to a stop in the middle of the abandoned street. "Neutral," I tell her, centering the stick and wiggling it a little.

"Oh, my God, Corbin. What if someone comes up behind us? They're going to nail us right in the ass!" she squawks, spinning to look out the back windshield.

"I'm going to nail you right in the ass if you don't chill and listen for a sec," I threaten, and her eyes come to me.

My right hand still on hers, I take it off the shifter and yank her across the center console, tangling my fingers in the back of her hair with my left. Her other hand comes to press into my chest for balance as I pull her face to mine and crush my lips to hers. I let my need for her show in this kiss. This isn't one of the sweet, innocent pecks she's used to. No. And it's more heated than any of the times we've made out since that first time I taught her how to French kiss.

Feeling her hand move up my chest, I breathe her in as she sighs, enjoying the combination of her watermelon-flavored drink mixed with something uniquely Vivian, and savor the touch of her fingers against my skin as she wraps them around the back of my neck, holding me to her. *Yes. God, yes.* This is what I've been waiting for. For months, all I've wanted was for her to show me she wants me just as badly as I want her, and finally, with her grip locked on, I now know for certain my girl will be all mine.

Just not right this second.

I let go of her hair and pull away slowly, so she doesn't feel rejected, and smile down into her beautiful face when I see her eyes are still closed, her breath coming out in short pants. "You ready, baby girl?" She nods, never lifting her lids, so I place her hand back on the stick shift, and tell her gently, "Then get us home."

She scoots back into her seat, lets out a deep breath, and finally opens her eyes, blinking a couple times to get her bearings. "Okay," she replies with another small nod.

"Over and up to first," I instruct, helping her with the first gear as I work the pedals to get us going. "Down to second." This time, she does it on her own, and when I coach, "Third," and she pushes it straight up flawlessly, I remove my hand and stretch my arm out to rest behind her shoulders.

I can't help the sense of pride I feel when I rev the engine, push in the clutch, and she moves the gear into fourth without my direction, and then finishes off with fifth the same way. She looks over at me with a beaming smile, obviously proud of herself too. "I'll have you driving stick in no time." A sound escapes her that's a cross between a hiccup, a giggle, and a snort, and I look at her in surprise. "Was... was your mind just in the gutter, baby girl?" I ask. "The one time I wasn't making a sexual innuendo...." I grin.

"You're rubbing off on me, I guess." She giggles sweetly.

"Not yet, but I will be."

BEFORE THE *lie*

EFORE THE *lie*

BEFORE THE *lie*

RE THE *lie*

lie

Ten

Vi

AFTER SHOWING THE GUARD at the gate our IDs, soon, we pulled into a parking lot between two huge, rectangular, four-story, plain beige buildings. The area was almost eerily silent. There were a ton of cars parked, but there wasn't a soul in sight.

"Where is everybody?" I whisper, the feel of the place making me want to be quiet and not disturb the silence.

"Half are deployed, and a lot are still out in the field for training. Only three of us come in at a time to guard the building, each taking a one-day shift and two days off, before we go back out in the woods," he explains.

As we walk in through the heavy-looking door, we pass an old metal desk that has a half-eaten meal in the center, but no one there to eat it. "This is where you spent all day yesterday?" I ask, and he nods, grabs my hand, and starts up the stairs. "No wonder you were bored out of your mind."

He doesn't reply, just continues to guide me up the four flights of stairs until we come out another metal door into a long, creepy hallway, a numbered, beige door breaking up the painted off-white cinderblock walls every eight feet or so. The lights must be motion-activated, because another buzzes on in the ceiling as we walk farther down the hall, and as I look behind me, I see the one closest to the stairwell door we exited through flicker back off. I hold Corbin's hand tighter in my right, and reach across my body to squeeze his bicep with my left, making him chuckle.

"Not gonna let anything get you, baby girl. These barracks are just old and decrepit, built in the 1950s," he soothes.

"All I'm hearing is 'This place is haunted as shit, and super old, so lots of years for ghosts to take up residence,'" I mumble, bring my side flush with his as he lets go of my hand and wraps his muscular arm around my back. I feel his fingers dig lightly into my ribs near my breast, and it sets off tingles throughout my body, doing an awesome job of distracting me from the scary setting we're in. And finally, he stops at a door, one that looks like all the other beige doors we've passed, only this one has a set of black numbers in the center: 308.

He takes his key out of his pocket, unlocks the door, and shoves it open, holding it for me to step through. When he lets go, it shuts on its own with a loud, echoing bang, making me jump. I try to shake off my nerves as I take in his home for the past two years. To the left, there is a giant wooden piece of furniture with a set of double doors. I don't know the proper name for it, but it's like an external closet. A wardrobe, I guess. It's kind of what I pictured when I read the Narnia books several years ago. Just past it, I can see about two feet of a bed covered in a fluffy blanket with an outdoor scene on it, and then another wardrobe at the foot of the bed. It makes me smile as I peek in.

"I used to do this with my bed," I tell him. "My mom would get frustrated with me, because I'd sneak off with all her pushpins out of her craft room and use them to attach sheets to the ceiling, like a canopy around my bed. It didn't work too well though, and they'd all end up falling after a couple hours. She finally got me one of those pretty sheer mosquito nets that hang down over the bed. I don't know. I just liked being in an enclosed space, kinda like little boys like to build forts, I guess."

The right side of his mouth tugs upward. "Totally get it, baby girl. It's the only way I can sleep. I feel too exposed otherwise. Also, it's for privacy. My roommate is deployed right now, but when he's here, he's a fucking chatty Kathy and wouldn't leave me alone before I arranged it like this," he explains, and I look farther into the room. Sure enough, past the second wardrobe is a twin-size bed along the back wall. Above it, I assume there is a window, but it is covered in a thick, black piece of fabric. In the center of it is an American flag attached with safety pins at the corners, and I can't help but smile. I love how proud and patriotic my soldier is. Looking to the right, there is a large dresser, with a good-sized TV on top with a DVD player next to it, and then yet another beige door.

"Is that the bathroom?" I ask, and he snorts.

"I wish. No. That's the next room over. We have latrines here," he says, and at my confused look, he adds, "Big shared bathroom down the hall. Kind of like in a locker room."

"Well crap," I grumble.

"What's up?"

"I definitely have to pee after all that watermelon Arizona drink and four hours in a car," I confess, fidgeting on my feet.

"There's nobody here. I'll take you down there." He opens the door, but I hesitate. "You coming?"

"I'm imagining a long wall of urinals and me trying to pee standing up."

"Soldiers still gotta take shits, Vi. There are two stalls with doors," he tells me, and I scrunch up my face, making him grin.

We only have to walk about ten feet down the creepy hallway before we reach the latrine, and I keep my eyes averted and head straight for the two stalls in the corner. Even though it's completely deserted, I still feel like I shouldn't be in here, since this is a place only men use during what would normally be private moments for civilians, using the bathroom and showering. I finish my business and quickly wash my hands at one of the faucets above the trough-style sink lining one of the walls. There's a metal shelf the length of it above the faucets for the men to place their toiletries while they shave and brush their teeth, or whatever else men do in the mirror.

As I step out into the hallway, I'm suddenly grabbed roughly from behind, and as I go to scream, panic flaring inside me, a hand clamps over my mouth. It's not until I smell Corbin's familiar, intoxicating scent, and then feel the fingers of his other hand begin to tickle my sides that I start to laugh, swinging my elbow behind me to get him back.

My back flush with his front, the heat of him sinks into my chilled bones, and as I laugh hysterically, wiggling against him, I'm no longer afraid of the unnerving old building. I stop fighting and let my body become dead-weight, and he stops his tickle torture and wraps his tattoo-covered arm around my narrow body beneath my breasts, holding me to him. He removes his hand from my mouth and uses it to pull my hair back so he can see the side of my face.

"Sorry, baby girl. I couldn't help it," he chuckles. "I wanted so bad to do that when we first got here, but I didn't want you to pee on me. Couldn't resist, knowing you had a freshly emptied bladder."

"You're a dick," I gasp, trying to catch my breath, but giggling still.

He laughs heartily then spins me around, making me squeak as he picks me up in his arms bridal-style and carries me back to his room and through the door, not stopping until he tosses me through the narrow opening onto his bed. "What do you want to watch?" he asks.

"What do you have?" I counter.

"As far as comedies," he begins, opening the top drawer of the dresser in the corner, "I have *Night at the Roxbury, A Knight's Tale, My Big Fat—*"

"*—Greek Wedding?* Yes! My favorite!" I exclaim, and he puts it into the DVD player, using the remote to turn on the TV as he walks back toward me. He tosses it onto the mattress next to me, and I watch, my eyes widening, as he grasps hold of the bottom of his T-shirt before pulling it off over his head in one quick motion. I gulp, taking in the perfection of his bare torso and arms.

He has a body the likes I've never seen on a real-life person. Maybe in fitness magazines, music videos, and action movies, but never up close, within reach. Sinewy forearms, bulging biceps, up to obscenely wide shoulders, fist-sized traps on either side of his strong neck, down to his pecs, wide and hard, but not overly big and puffed up like I've seen on some body builders. They're proportioned to the rest of him, the perfect canvas for his vibrant chest piece, the vivid green-and-red snake battling the black eagle, the beak of its white head about to take a chomp out of the long, slithering body.

My eyes trail downward, over the six perfectly symmetrical protruding abs, a deep trench between the two columns leading my gaze even farther south, to the V-shaped muscles above his hips. *Jesus, is he even real?*

He takes a pace forward, and I fight the urge to move back on the bed, instead holding my seated position on the edge as he uses his knee to separate both of mine and steps between my now spread legs. My heart thumps, and I stare straight ahead into that flawless tattoo, unable to look up to meet his eyes. My hands tremble where they clench the edge of the mattress, and I can't seem to inhale.

His hand comes up beneath my chin, and as he lifts it, my lids close on their own. My stomach clenches as I feel him press closer, his body coming into contact with my most intimate place, and I finally suck in a breath just as his mouth presses to mine. His palm lowers to the base of my throat, and it's a much lower part of my body that clenches this time, as his hand rests there, firm and hot, sending a thrill down my spine. Using pressure against my sternum, he lays me back on the bed, his lips never leaving mine as his tongue slips between them, and his other hand comes down at the side of my head to brace him. Just like the kiss in his car, I melt into him, following his lead and losing myself as his tongue dances with mine. Without a spoken word, he teaches me ways to draw out the most pleasure, and unconsciously my hips begin to move against him, my core suddenly needing... something. I don't know what.

The hand at my throat starts to move downward, his fingers spreading wide as he slides over the center of my chest and stomach until he reaches the hem of my shirt. He tugs it up, and I swallow but bravely help him pull it off me, finally breaking our kiss. I hold my breath as he looks down at the lacy light gray bralette that covers my small breasts, watching his face heat and his eyes turn stormy. But the gentleness of his touch that follows doesn't match the aggression I sense just beneath the surface, and I can tell he's holding himself in check so as to not scare me.

With the tips of his fingers of his right hand, he traces the edge of the lace over the gentle swell of my breast, and as they reach the clasp at the center of the flimsy cups, he unhooks it effortlessly, letting them fall open and to the sides of my body. I feel lightheaded, realizing I haven't exchanged the oxygen out of my lungs in a while, and I see his eyes follow the movement as my chest expands then relaxes. The dark chocolate pools staring so intently at me make me squirm, and to make it stop, I reach up to grab the back of Corbin's neck, trying to force him down to kiss me again. But he doesn't budge. The only thing that moves is his gaze as he raises it to meet mine.

"So fucking perfect, baby girl," he growls, and my gut tightens.

"N-no one's ever seen me naked before, Corbin. You're making me nervous just staring at me like that," I whisper.

"I could just stare at you for the rest of the night, Vi. You're so goddamn beautiful." He lowers his face to the center of my chest then trails his nose across my skin, making it prickle and hardening my nipples. When he exchanges the soft touch with the roughness of his stubbled cheek, I shudder, my arms coming up to encircle his shoulders, my hands clasping behind his shaved head. When he finally takes one nipple into his mouth, I let out a loud moan, the sound surprising me, and I clamp down on my bottom lip in embarrassment.

He must hear the abrupt way I cut off the noise, because he stops what he was doing, leans up over my face, and uses his thumb to pull my lip free. "Don't ever silence yourself when I'm giving you pleasure. There's no sexier sound than one that comes out of you, letting me know I'm making you feel good." The tone of his voice sounds like both a command and a reassurance, and all I can do is nod.

Before I know what's happening, his strong arm shoves between my lower back and the mattress, I'm moving, and my head is suddenly lying on his pillow, his scent filling my lungs as he lowers himself on his elbows, one on either side of my head, as his body comes to lie between my legs. The weight of him on top of me is both comforting and thrilling, and I fight the urge to move beneath him like a cat seeking attention. His face lowers to my neck, kissing up to my ear until he takes the lobe between his teeth, making me whimper.

My hands come up to grasp at his back as he drives me into a frenzy, his mouth doing magical things as he trails his tongue back down to my breast, the one that hadn't received his earlier attention. This time, I don't stop myself as the moan escapes me, and I'm rewarded with a thrust of his hips against my pulsating center.

He travels farther down, and when he reaches the top of my jeans, I tell myself to keep breathing as he undoes the button and zipper, leaning back on his knees to pull them down and off, leaving me in nothing but the light gray lace panties that match my bralette. Instead of focusing on his eyes, devouring me like I'm a buffet and he hasn't eaten in days, I decide to take in his glorious body, in perfect view as he rests his ass back on his heels between my thighs. For the first time in my life, I feel sexy, desirable, because if a man who looks the way Corbin does is gazing at me like he's contemplating which part to consume first, then I'm not going to worry about my body anymore.

So it's with this thought in mind that when he takes hold of the lace at my hips and sweeps it down my legs then onto the floor, I try not to react. I feel my knees involuntarily begin to close, wanting to protect the place between them, but Corbin stops their movement with palms to my inner thighs, making them move in the opposite direction as he opens me up farther than I was to begin with. I close my eyes as he lowers himself there, feeling his massive, hard shoulders against the soft part at the backs of my thighs.

"Breathe, baby girl," he says against the inside of my legs, as he begins to kiss his way downward.

I inhale, grasping at the sheets beneath me, not knowing what to do as he gets closer and closer to the place that needs his touch so badly. And without further torture, the anticipation nearly killing me, I feel the first lap of his tongue against my flesh and shudder, my whole body trying to close in on itself, but Corbin wraps his hands around the base of my thighs, where they connect to the rest of me, keeping my hips steady as he begins to devour me. There's no other way to describe what he's doing, as he doesn't just flick his tongue against my clit. No, he covers and consumes me with his whole mouth, the sounds almost obscene but undeniably sexy as he eats me.

There would have been no way to hold back my cries of

pleasure, even if I wanted to. Never have I felt anything like what he's doing to me. Is this why it was so shocking to Corbin and Sierra when they found out I've never masturbated? Is this what it felt like just by touching down there? Surely not. I have a feeling nothing I could do to myself would ever feel as all-consuming as this. I feel every stroke of his talented tongue from the roots of my hair down to the tips of my toes, which curl then flex, as I'm unable to keep myself still.

And suddenly, something starts to build inside me. As if I've begun running up a hill, climbing my way to the top. It's almost frightening in its intensity, and I'm not sure what I'll find once I make it to the peak. But as his grip tightens on my legs when I squirm, and his mouth keeps up its relentless rhythm, the runner inside me gets an unexpected burst of energy and starts sprinting toward her finish line.

Abruptly, every muscle in my body seizes, tightening to an almost painful degree, and my breath catches in my chest as a sudden explosion goes off inside me and I call out his name on a sob. I fold in on myself, trying to curl into a fetal position around Corbin's upper body before my limbs and everything inside me goes lax, feeling like I've turned into liquid as he takes one final lap from bottom to top. A shudder runs through me as he presses a kiss to my clit, and then he crawls up my body, hovering over me as I pant, my heart feeling like it's beating so hard it's going to levitate right out of my chest while the rest of me melts into the mattress beneath me.

But before I can even come down from my high, I feel Corbin between my legs, and I open my eyes to glance down and see his hand disappear at the apex of my thighs just as I feel his finger enter me. My back bows off the bed at the pleasurable intrusion, bringing me up against the hard muscles of his torso. Then his lips cover mine before his tongue dips between them, mimicking what his finger is doing inside me. I moan into his mouth, tasting my own flavor for the first time, finding it oddly sexy. Soon, I'm almost uncomfortably full as a second finger joins the first, so I concentrate on what his mouth is doing to mine, whimpering as he presses them deep then sweeps them across my inner walls.

"I've gotta get you ready for me, baby girl. Just relax. Let me make you feel good," he breathes against my lips. "So fucking tight, but you're so wet for me. God, you're going to feel like a fist around my cock."

His words make me clamp around his fingers, and we both groan. He leans down, his face going into the side of my neck, and suddenly a sense of calm washes over me, being completely surrounded by Corbin. With his tongue tracing up the column to my ear, while his hand that's not working magic inside my soaking-wet heat braces him on the other side of my head, I'm enveloped by an art-covered wall of muscle. My inner muscles relax as I breathe in his familiar, comforting scent as his teeth send tingles through my extremities when they clamp down on my earlobe. I shiver and feel my nipples tighten against his rock-hard chest, my hips beginning to move against his knuckles.

My breathing becomes heavy again, and just as that feeling starts to build inside me once more, he pulls his fingers away, and my eyes shoot open in confusion. But then I look down, seeing him use the wetness on his hand to spread over the head of his erection. My heart thumps, knowing what this means, and I'm both nervous yet anxious for it to happen.

"Stay relaxed, baby girl," he whispers in my ear, the heat of his breath making goose bumps prickle across my skin, but I consciously try to do what he instructs.

I watch as he uses his hand to line up the bulbous head with my center before taking one of my hands in his grip, bring it above my head before doing the same with the other. His elbows then press into the mattress at the sides of my head for balance, and I relax even further as he cages me in, my small breasts pressed against his chest as my arms are stretched up the pillow. He laces his fingers together with mine, as he tells me clearly, "I'm clean. Got tested the week I met you, and there's been no one since. I've never been with anyone without a condom before, but I'll be damned if anything is between us when I take you for the first time. Do you trust me?"

Without hesitation, I nod, and my fingers squeeze between his as I feel him slowly start to ease inside me.

"Breathe, Vi. Don't hold it in, my love," he commands gently, and his use of the word steals all the oxygen out of my lungs before I inhale once again as he sinks deeper. "Look at me. I want to see those beautiful eyes while I finally make you mine."

When my eyes meet his, they feel like they lock into place, and I'm unable to look away, even as they fill with tears as my core starts to burn. It's not the pleasant heat that had blazed there before, when the new sensation of need had sparked. No. It's the fiery sensation of tearing as he presses ahead, breaking through the bit of flesh that is the only thing separating us from becoming one entity.

But even as I whimper at the pain, my gaze stays locked on his, and I focus on the look of pleasure and concentration in those chocolaty depths. And when he's completely seated inside me, the weight of him fitting perfectly between my thighs, only then does he lean down to kiss me ever so gently, staying perfectly still to allow the hurt to dissipate. He trails kisses over my jaw and up to my ear, flicking his tongue across a sensitive spot just below it, then he whispers, "You tell me when to move, baby girl. I'd stay like this all night, so fucking happy just to finally be inside you. I won't move an inch. Won't cause you any more pain, only pleasure from here on out."

His words cause me to flex around his steel shaft, and an amazing sensation shoots from my center outward, making me gasp. He lifts himself to look into my face once again, and his eyes go soft, seeing nothing but desire written there. I nod, unable to speak, but he understands me nonetheless.

He begins to move, and everything around us fades to black as every one of my senses zero in on where Corbin's and my body are joined. My hands relax and flex in his, and I struggle to tug them free, having an urgent need to curl myself around him as he thrusts. He gives in, letting go, and I immediately wrap my arms around his torso, grasping onto the deep trench of muscle at the center of his back. It brings our bodies flush together, and his face goes back into my neck where he breathes me in deeply then lets out a sexy groan that has me shuddering beneath him.

"Never felt anything so perfect, Vi," he whispers. "Made for me." He stops his rhythm and sinks all the way in for a moment, grinding his hips. "I can feel where you end. The head of my cock is kissing it. Right... there." He presses even deeper, and I moan, feeling him against what must be my cervix. My nails sink into his back and he sucks in air, thrusting hard and making me cry out. "God, baby girl. You're going to have to retract those claws, because you're not ready for what that does to me." His eyes gleam with something I don't understand. I relax my hands, moving them beneath his arms to wrap up and grip onto his shoulders instead.

He returns to his smooth, rhythmic pulses, his body moving in a sensual dance above me. I wish there was a mirror anchored to the ceiling, that way I could watch from a distance what he looks like as he brings me pleasure I never knew existed. So closely pressed against me, I feel every one of his muscles working, but I bet the actual sight of seeing them ripple as his body rolls and thrusts would be glorious and overwhelmingly erotic.

Suddenly, his legs are no longer stretched out behind him, where I'd previously had my ankles wrapped around his calves. Instead, he brings the massive trunks beneath him to rest on his knees as he wraps his arm around my lower back, elevating my hips. This new angle causes him to rub something inside me that has me moaning in pleasure, my legs clamping around his hips as his tempo begins to speed up.

But as good as it feels now, the pain completely gone except for when he goes just a little too deep, that building feeling doesn't return, no matter how hard I concentrate. My eyes closed, my brow furrowed, my front teeth clamping down on my bottom lips, I start to get frustrated that the runner inside me hasn't begun to make her journey up the hill.

Being so in tune with me, Corbin's arm tightens around my body, and his bicep squeezes my upper back, lifting me up to him so tight I can feel our hearts beating against each other. "Relax, baby girl. It probably won't happen this time. A virgin never comes her first time. But I swear I'm going to take care of you. Not going to last much longer. You just feel too perfect." He groans into my neck as he circles his hips, and I do as he says, relaxing and enjoying the sensations he's setting off inside me instead of chasing the orgasm I thought was supposed to come.

In all the romances novels I read, the virgin heroine always came after the hero broke her 'maidenhead.' But his words make me feel better, understanding nothing is wrong with me, and I melt into him as his thrusts become more powerful.

With my breath coming out in forced gusts that match his every plunge, his muscles suddenly tighten, and he squeezes my small body to him so close that for a moment I can't tell where I end and he begins before he swiftly pulls out, spilling his hot liquid onto my stomach.

Keeping his hips elevated, as not to smear his cum between us, he lowers my upper body back to the pillow, kissing me gently as we both catch our breath. I look up into his eyes, seeing a look that matches what he called me when he first entered me, but I don't say anything, even though I feel exactly what his expression is telling me without words. He smiles down at me, his perfect, straight white teeth flashing, making my heart skip, and then he glances down our bodies before looking up at me once more.

"Don't look, baby girl," he orders quietly. Normally, if anyone else would tell me that, my automatic reaction would be to do the exact opposite. But being Corbin, and the way I naturally want to do exactly as he says, my eyes stay locked on his. They twinkle, looking happier and more carefree than I've ever seen him, and it makes my soul twirl that I did that to him. "I'm going to go get you a wet washcloth to clean up my mess. It looks like I *avada kedavra*'d your pussy." He chuckles.

"What?" I gasp, and just as I start to glance down at myself, he catches my chin and locks a more serious look with mine.

"Don't. Look," he commands. "It's not a big deal, Vi. Just a little blood and a shit load of cum. I'll be right back." He kisses me once more before backing up off the bed, wrapping a towel around his hips that had been laying across his dresser. He disappears behind the wardrobe, and I hear the door open and shut. I lie there, and force myself to obey his order, taking comfort from the fact he had been so nonchalant about it.

He returns moments later, and as I reach out for the slightly steaming washcloth in his hand, he bats it away, shaking his head. "It's my job to take care of you, my love," he murmurs, and everything inside me goes soft as he begins to carefully clean between my legs. When he's finished there, he wipes away the liquid on my stomach before folding the mess up inside the cloth then sets it somewhere out of sight.

When he comes back, I expect him to lie down next to me, but instead, he positions himself between my legs once more, placing my calves over his shoulders. I tug the pillow above me to beneath my head and peek down at him as he trails gentle kisses down my still-trembling thigh. He must feel my eyes on him, because his lift and lock on mine, his intense stare sending a chill down my spine as he continues his path to my center.

When he reaches his target, he hovers there, his breath the only thing he touches me with, but as sensitive as I am right now, I feel it as clearly as if he were stroking me with his tongue. His gaze too penetrating, my lids close and I turn my face away, becoming suddenly embarrassed as he watches his effect on me. But he growls, and somehow I know it's his unspoken order to return my eyes to him.

"Good girl," he murmurs, his hot breath on my core making me moan as much as his praise. And what he says next, turns my world upside down. "I love you, Vi. Have since before I even actually saw you. That feeling I told you about, the one I had when you were walking up to the front of the gym to give me the belay lesson that first day? I swear, baby girl. That was my soul finding its mate. It was so shocking, because I truly didn't think I even had a soul, knowing all the bad shit I've done in my life. And I don't deserve you. I *know* I don't fucking deserve someone so sweet, and beautiful, and *good*. But I promise, I'll spend every day for the rest of my life trying to be a man worthy of you."

With tears in my eyes, and before I can respond, without warning, his scorching mouth covers me, and all thoughts of replying to his heartfelt confession twirls to the back of my mind. Instead of being too overwhelming as I thought it would be, being so sensitive, the heat of his mouth is actually soothing, and my tense muscles relax as he does exactly what he promised before he orgasmed—takes care of me like no one ever has.

BEFORE THE *li*

EFORE THE *lie*

BEFORE THE *lie*

RE THE *lie*

lie

Eleven

Corbin

TIME.

It used to move so slowly.

I can remember when I was a kid, being bored out of my mind at home. Trying to pass the time by playing video games or outside with friends in my neighborhood in California.

School days moved at a snail's pace, each period seeming to last for hours, my nonexistent attention span making the time spent in a classroom a slow form of torture.

Or a few years later, after my babysitter introduced me to her friend, who eventually oversaw my initiation into the gang. Time had virtually stood still between the second I lifted my booted foot above the back of a rival gang member's head, and then the next, as it connected with his skull, breaking his jaw where his teeth were clamped down on the sidewalk's cement curb.

The fifteen-minute drive in the back of the police car after I got caught stealing from the liquor store when I was seventeen felt more like a year, not knowing what my future held.

Boot camp. God. From the second I sat in the barber chair for them to shave off all my hair that first time, until I stepped off the bus in Ft. Vanter after it was complete, it was the slowest point in my life. After living as what I thought was a hard-ass in an unstoppable gang that didn't have to follow rules, basic training was a whole new world. One full of drill sergeants who made it their life goal to break me. And they eventually did. Those ten weeks felt like a decade.

But on this night, as I look down at the ring inside the velvet box in my hand, I think back to the first time I made love to Vi, now seven months ago. Time has absolutely flown by. That's not to say there haven't been times when the hours, days, and weeks didn't crawl by, like when I was in the field just a few months into our relationship, or the three weeks I spent at Non-Commissioned Officer school, before I earned my rank as a sergeant back in July. But it seems like just yesterday I took her virginity on the same night I gave her my confession. I love her. I've never loved anyone before, but I know without a shadow of a doubt that I love Vivian.

And God does that girl love the shit out of me. She still looks at me like I hung all those damn stars. She still responds to my touch like it's the very first time. And for once in my life, I truly trust someone to the depths of my soul.

There is a part of me I haven't fully shown her yet. The part that still wants to protect her and keep her safe, but at the same time use her small, almost fragile body in ways that would scare someone as sweet and innocent as her. I fantasize about adding pain to her pleasure, dominating her in ways other than with my commands, which she still follows without batting a lash. I don't think she even realizes she's following an order when I give her one. My control over her is a subtle thing, one we've never talked about, having always just been there. And since everything I've always told her to do has been for nothing other than bringing her more pleasure, or keeping her safe, or improving something in her life—like when I taught her to drive, then eventually took her to get her license, before surprising her with a Chevy Malibu for her birthday two months ago—she's never had a reason to bring it up.

But it feels so good being a man who Vi deserves, a fierce yet affectionate protector for my doting and faithful lover, that I haven't minded putting that part of me aside. Keeping her is worth more than fulfilling my darker needs.

At last, her family arrives, the bell above the door jingling as it always has. Vi looks over her shoulder for a moment from where she was marking rocks with her stick of chalk, a route she's dying to try that her boss was telling her the climbing coach couldn't even beat, and I hide the ring box back in my shorts' pocket.

A look of confusion registers on her face when her mom and dad walk into the rock gym, and it quickly turns into surprise when her brother comes in behind them. "Henry?" she cries, and takes off running across the gym. I watch, a smile splitting my face when I see her launch herself at him before he catches her. "What are you doing here?" Her voice is shrill in her excitement, and it carries throughout the entire building.

I see Sierra pop her head out of the office. She looks at Vi before her eyes come to meet mine, and I give her a slight nod, giving her the signal. A grin covers her face before she disappears again, and just as Henry stops next to me on the couch, carrying Vi as he followed their parents, I stand, and all the lights in the gym go out.

"What the...?" Vi whispers, and she reaches out to grasp hold of my forearm, sensing exactly where I am without having to see me. I pull the blindfold out of my pocket then trail the hand of the arm opposite of the one she's holding, up from her hand, all the way to her shoulder, feeling her skin prickle. When I reach her neck, I pull her closer to me before lifting both my hands to place the blindfold over her head then down to cover her eyes. "Corbin, what's going on?"

Vi doesn't see it, but Sierra flips the switch that turns on all the newly hung blacklights around the gym. Vi had a genius idea about a month ago to install them and coat the walls with invisible paint that only shows up under a blacklight. Now, Rock On offers birthday parties and lock-ins, where you can climb on the glowing walls. She got the idea after I took her cosmic bowling, told Sierra about it, and the owners approved. They even offered her a cut of every birthday party and lock-in sold.

I take her hands in mine and look at her family, all three of them giving me an encouraging nod, her mom's hands coming up to cover her mouth, as tears flood her eyes. Sierra comes to stand next to them, the biggest grin on her face. She and Vi have become close over the past several months, and I'm so happy that my girl has such a great friend. She'll need all the support she can get, for when I go to Ranger school next cycle, and when I get deployed.

Taking a deep breath, I give her the short but meaningful speech I've been rehearsing in my head since last week, when

I asked her dad's permission to ask Vi to marry me. "Vivian, something inside me recognized you before I ever laid eyes on you, and as I told you that day I confessed I'd fallen in love with you, I believe it was my soul finding its other half. From that very second, I went with my gut. For once in my life, I listened to my heart. And now, I'm using my brain, because for the first time in all twenty-one years I've been on this earth, my head is screwed on right, and it's all because of you. And what all four of those parts are telling me to do is to snatch you up before anyone else can try to steal you away from me, before you realize you are way too good for me." I lean close to her ear, whispering for only her to hear, "Keyword, *try*. Because I'd kill any motherfucker who ever attempted."

When I pull back, she's biting her lip, her natural reaction any time I say something that turns her on, and I thank God she finds my possessiveness sexy, because that's one part of me I'll never be able to push aside. I get down on one knee and let go of her hands to take the ring box out of my pocket, opening it up. Then I reach up and tug down her blindfold.

When she opens her eyes, she looks up first, her mouth falling open as she reads what's painted on the wall behind me. The very one she had been marking with her chalk not five minutes ago and had no idea it had been repainted. Glowing there in bright purple—a nice touch suggested by Sierra, knowing it's Vi's favorite color—the wall now reads, *Will you marry me, Spidergirl?*

She then looks down at me, seeing the ring I'm holding up to her, and her hands shoot up to cover her gaping mouth, a younger version of her mom standing in the exact same pose behind her. And then she launches herself at me, able to knock me backward in my unbalanced position on one knee, and lands on top of me. We land with an *oomph,* and as everyone laughs, she sobs a, "Yes!" before kissing me.

And with a grin, I let myself soak in the moment, her family and best friend cheering behind us, as I realize... after almost a year together, *she* finally kissed *me.*

The End of Our Story...

Before the Lie

Epilogue

The Lie
2 years later...

THE PHONE RINGS AND MY heart thumps painfully, seeing the unknown number. Three days have passed since I last spoke to my husband, the love of my life. He's been deployed to Afghanistan for four months now. He calls me when he can, normally every three days, when we'll sit and talk to each other for the allotted twenty minutes, usually just repeating over and over how much we love and miss each other, and how we can't wait for the deployment to end so he can come home and make love to me, hold me, see me in person instead of just pictures.

"H-hello?" I breathe, my hand trembling as it holds my cell to my ear, and I close my eyes as Corbin's deep voice comes through the line.

"Hi, baby girl. You okay?" he asks, hearing my stutter instead of my usual chipper greeting of 'Hey, honey!'

I take a deep breath, ready to spew the lies I've rehearsed over and over in my head, feeling in my heart it's the best decision. If Corbin knew the truth... God. He'd lose it—his composure, his sanity... his freedom. He'd go to jail for the rest of his life for going after the man who has ruined mine, my chance at living a happily ever after. Or he'd lose his life if my attacker was somehow miraculously able to get a one-up on Corbin. There's no other way. I have to lie.

"No, baby. I'm not okay," I answer, my voice weak, quivering.

"What's happened? Is your mom all right? Babe, talk to me," he urges, panic starting to fill his normally strong, unwavering timbre.

"Something... something happened at Sierra's neighbor's party. I—"

"What party?" he interrupts, and I close my eyes.

"Sierra's neighbor had a going away party. They're deploying with her husband, who's already over there. She invited me to go with her, wanting to get me out of the house," I explain. The one truth in this dreaded conversation.

"Okay, what happened?" he repeats.

"We were all drinking. I had too many to drive home, so I stayed with Sierra and her roommate. I... I did something *horrible*," my voice cracks on the last word. It wasn't me who'd done the most vile act anyone could possibly do to a person besides murder them. A sob escapes my throat before I can stop it.

"Baby... what are you saying? What did you do?" he prompts,

confusion clear in his tone.

He's the man of my dreams. My soul mate. There's no way he would think I'd cheat on him, so he won't read between the lines himself. I have to actually say the untruthful words. I have to let them come out of my mouth, even though I would never do that to anyone. Especially not to the man who is the center of my universe. But I have to make him believe it.

Why not just keep it a secret? a voice inside my head suggests. The same suggestion it's offered up countless times over the last seventy-two hours. But I can't. There's no way I'd be able to make love to my husband, knowing someone else had been inside me—however unwanted—without him being aware of it. The guilt would eat me alive. No, this would be best. I'd tell him I'd made a mistake, he'd forgive me, and then he could just move past it. It would only be my burden to bear, no extra weight on his shoulders. He has enough to deal with, over there fighting for his country.

"I was drunk. I... I slept with someone." There. The lie is out. An equal mix of relief and shame sweeps over me, making me dizzy, so I sit down on the edge of our bed. Opening my eyes to look at the picture of us on our nightstand, the image goes blurry as tears fill them to the brim.

He doesn't say anything at first, but I can hear his breathing become rapid. My tears overflow and spill down my cheeks. Dear God, what have I done? I've hurt him. I've hurt the man I promised to protect and love for the rest of my life. I feel my heart break as he gulps audibly on the other end of the line. If he's anything like me, he's feeling sick to his stomach, swallowing back the bile that wants to spew from its depths.

"Ba—" I start, but I think better of it. I'm sure he doesn't want me calling him any terms of endearment. "Corbin. Say something."

It's then that I recall the one thing he always told me. From day one. Even reiterating it in our wedding vows. *Just stay loyal, and I'll always be yours, baby girl.* And even though I should have seen it coming, when he finally speaks, I shatter.

"I'll have the divorce papers sent to you."

And the phone goes dead.

You can join my reader group,
KD-Rob's Mob, here:
https://www.facebook.com/groups/361767417319236/

Note from the Author:

When I sat down to write Truth Revealed, I didn't know where to begin. I knew it was going to be a second-chance romance, but there was so much to Corbin and Vi's start that I didn't believe flashbacks within the one book would do it justice. Therefore, I decided to tell their first story through a novella... but then that novella turned into a full-length novel, and so now we have *Before the Lie.*

Truth Revealed is the tale that actually originally popped into my head. Yet it wasn't until I began to plot out how their second chance at love would go that I realized nothing would make sense unless I told everyone about their beautiful then tragic beginnings. Although painful to write for personal reasons, I'm hoping that in knowing their story, Part 2 in the Confession Duet will be all the sweeter in its vengeance.

One last thing I should mention: Although Matthew inspired Corbin's looks and a lot of his personality, he allowed me to make up stories about his tattoos. And just so we're clear, sweet yet badass Turd was never in a gang in California, nor did he join the military because he was given the choice between it or jail. #merica

Acknowledgements

Matthew Hosea, thank you for helping me with so much of the hero in this book, and for being the—really, really ridiculously good-looking—face of Corbin. Thank you for your infallible support when I got scared to put this story down on paper. It's heavy and scary, but as always, you lent me your strength and courage to put it out there. I don't know what I would do without your belief in me. Love you, Turd. #nerdandturd

My Hot Tree girls, Bec, Barb, Mandy, and Tina, thank y'all for all the work you did on BTL. It was rough for me to write outside my romantic comedy voice, and your notes and tweaks helped me so much. And Sierra, for your unique way of making me feel like I am somebody special. Y'all's tears made my soul happy. *evil grin

Finally, DB. Thank you for reading, even though you claim you don't know how. You'll always be a hero in my eyes.

Coming Soon

Truth Revealed

Confession Duet Book 2

It's been a decade since the woman who was the love of my life, my wife, confessed to cheating on me while I was deployed.

Ten years since I divorced her.

Ten years since I spoke to Vi, my soul mate, the girl who had brought me to life only to stab me in the heart, sending me into an even darker state than where I was before I met her.

Ten years, I've been watching her from afar, keeping tabs.

After a decade in the Army, two Purple Hearts and a Medal of Honor under my belt, I was kicked out with an honorable discharge, knowing no other skill than One Shot One Kill. Two years later, I'm part of a group of mercenaries who carry out justice. Criminals who hide behind their fancy lawyers and power—we take care of them and make it all look like karma. And with intel from our founder, Dr. Walker, a therapist with a long list of predators whose victims were too scared to turn them in, work is plenty and fulfilling.

Until Vi begins her sessions and I discover the reality I've lived the past ten years was nothing but a lie, when the truth is revealed.

CPSIA information can be obtained
at www.ICGtesting.com
Printed in the USA
LVOW13s0616121017
552144LV00017B/476/P

9 781541 345263